THE SECOND CHANCE

SAFA SALSABEEL Z

Contents

Contents

Preface

"What if the power to heal lies not in the world we know, but in the world we dream?"

This question has haunted me, guided me, and ultimately shaped the very heart of this novel. Through the pages that follow, I invite you into a story that begins with a girl, Riya, whose life has been defined by tragedy, yet who seeks something far greater than what fate has given her. In a world where scars are seen as flaws, Riya's story unfolds in a way you might never expect where the impossible becomes the only way forward.

As a student of English Literature, I've often been captivated by the power of words, stories, and the worlds we can create with them. Writing has always been my escape, my way of navigating the depths of human emotion, and understanding the complexities of life. Each sentence is an exploration, each word a brushstroke painting the portrait of a world unseen.

This novel is the culmination of my own journey, a journey where writing became not just a passion, but a lifeline. It is my first attempt at capturing the essence of pain, healing, and transformation through the lens of fiction. And as you read, I hope you find yourself lost in the mystery of Riya's dreams, drawn into the questions that challenge not just her existence, but ours.

Is it possible for our dreams to reshape our reality? Can we truly rewrite the narratives of our lives, even the most painful ones? This is a question I don't just want to answer, but one I want you to explore with me, step by step, page by page.

Thank you for picking up this book, for taking a chance on this first journey of mine. I hope, as you turn the pages, you feel the same sense of happiness and fulfillment that writing has brought to me.

Acknowledgements

Healing isn't always found in the world we see, it often emerges from the spaces we dream of, the stories we tell ourselves, and the hope we hold onto. This novel isn't just a story; it's a journey through pain, resilience, and the quiet magic of transformation. At its heart is Riya, a young woman whose life has been shaped by loss but who refuses to be defined by it. In a world that often mistakes scars for weakness. Her journey proves that sometimes, the impossible is just another path forward.

As a student of English Literature, I've always been drawn to the way words can shape worlds, how they can heal, challenge, and inspire. Writing has never been just a craft for me it's been a refuge, a way to make sense of emotions that are sometimes too big to name. This book is a piece of that journey, my maiden attempt at capturing the rawness of loss, the beauty of healing, and the strength found in transformation. As you turn these pages, I hope you not only follow Riya's journey but also find pieces of yourself within it.

This book wouldn't exist without the people who believed in me. I wish to thank my parents, whose unwavering love and faith in me have been my anchor.

A floral and profound thanks to prof.Dr. Samuel Rufus, whose wisdom, support, and passion for literature have shaped not just this book but also the way I see stories and life itself. His guidance has been invaluable and consistent. I would also like to extend my sincere gratitude to all my professors, whose knowledge, encouragement, and mentorship have played a significant role in shaping my academic and creative journey.

A special thanks to Reji Jacob for meticulously proofreading my work, ensuring that every sentence carries the weight and clarity it was meant to. I'm also incredibly grateful to Nitish Kumar RK for his keen eye and patience in editing this novel.I also extend my heartfelt gratitude to Dhanush Kumar who helped a lot for this book.

And to you, the reader 'Thank you'. This book is for You, for the dreamers, the seekers, the ones who believe that stories can heal. As you walk through these pages, you will find a sense of wonder and connection with this story.

CHAPTER ONE

SHATTERED LIGHT

The room was draped in shadow, heavy with a spooky atmosphere that enveloped the walls. Riya sat alone in the suffocating darkness of her room. A single beam of light dared to enter through the gap in the red curtains, lighting the chaos within. Pieces of shattered glass lay scattered across the floor. In one of the broken shards, her half-burnt face was mirrored, a haunting image of despair. Half of her face was scarred by the harsh embrace of flames.

The golden hue fell on the shattered mirror. The fractured glass caught the glow, scattering it over the floor in fragmented patterns, as if trying to piece together a story it could no longer tell. In its reflection, Riya's face appeared half bathed in light, half lost in shadow. Half of her face was soft and flawless, a quick reminder of what once was. The other side, however, bore the painful scars of fire which had stolen more than her skin.

Her eyes were black as coal, heavy with silent weight of a million unvoiced thoughts. She sat in complete stillness, the image of herself felt like a shackle around her chest pulling her down. The light seemed to mock her, illuminating only the things she wished to hide, while the darkness around her refused to offer solace.

The bits of glass at her feet caught the dim light, shining like tiny, sharp pieces of glitters. She sat there swallowed by the night and the maze of emotions, the silence pierced, as though the room itself wept for her sorrow. She sealed the curtains shut, silencing the last rays of the light. Darkness consumed the room entirely and once more the dim reflection of her fractured being was her only companion. Her voice cracked in a scream, carrying the ache of lost hope, heavy with despair and haunting ache of lost memories. She stumbled to the bathroom, her legs weak, her steps slow. Yet again, she shrieked again, which shattered the silence echoing off the cold tiled walls. It was a cry from deep down, like something way beyond just physical pain.

She couldn't erase the memories that kept haunting her which constantly resurfaced. The hands, the force, the helplessness. She was frozen, paralyzed, and trapped by the violation, her once bright dreams of becoming a doctor drowned in an ocean of despair. It wasn't just her life that had been shattered that day it was her soul, her aspirations, her belief in the goodness of the world. The spark of confidence that once glimmered in her eyes had faded into shadow of hollow misery.

Her parents too were submerged in sorrow. Her mother Anita, the beacon of strength, her source of resilience, now stood dimmed and broken. Though she tried her best to comfort Riya. She was fading into the murky depths of desolation. The knocks on her door went unanswered, the calls from friends ignored.

Her phone kept ringing, desperate for attention. This time, Riya finally picked up, there was silence on both ends. Her best friend, Sandhya, broke the silence, her voice hesitant but determined. "Riya," her voice filled with concern, "What's going on?"

Riya's body shook with terror, her lips trembled with fear as she struggled to speak. Rather than words, a strangled wail broke free from her, raw and unedited. Sandhya's heart raced, the weight of something being terribly wrong pressing on her.

"I'm coming to you..." Sandhya said, her voice resolute. Riya didn't respond, but Sandhya had made up her mind. She was already on her way.

As Sandhya stepped into Riya's home a suffocating silence greeted her. The air felt charged with unshed emotions. The sorrow in the air was almost tangible. Riya's mother, pale and tear-stricken opened the door. Her lips trembled as she struggled to form words, "She is upstairs", Riya's mother whispered in a heavy tone. Without a second thought, Sandhya hurried passed and climbed the stairs, her anxiety mounting with each step. She knocked frantically on Riya's door shouting her name. The silence on the other side was agonizing, the door creaked opened to reveal a sight far more devastating than she had dared to imagine. The room was engulfed in darkness, suffused with an overwhelming sense of despair. Sandhya flicked on the light, illuminating a scene of heart-breaking chaos. Riya stood in the centre her face partially burnt, her neck bearing deep scars, her thin frame barely holding up. Around her the floor was a chaotic mess of ripped clothes, broken glass and smudges of makeup smeared beyond identity. On the wall, an upside-down world map hung, a cruel and bitter symbol of disrupted reality.

'Riya!' Sandhya whispered, her voice was breaking. Riya sat motionless, her lips remained sealed, her gaze fixed on the floor. Her body language screamed of trauma, her silence a shield against the world. Sandhya inched closer, her hands shaking as she reached to comfort her and Sandhya said softly, "What happened to you? Talk to me."

The stillness stretched on thick with unspoken words. Then, drawing a breath that shook with emotion, Riya softly uttered, "It's all because of him." Sandhya spoke with a gentle caution her thoughts swirling with questions, "Who is it?" she asked softly. Without uttering a single word, Riya picked up a torn piece of paper and with shaky fingers, wrote down the name 'Mukesh'.

The name of the paper sent an icy chill through Sandhya's body. Every word was a stab to Sandhya's heart. Riya's story unfolded like a nightmare, one of trust betrayed and innocence stolen. Mukesh had been someone she thought she could trust, a family who had walked freely into their lives. And then, in a single horrific moment, he had torn apart everything she held dear.

While Sandhya listened, her fists clenched, her frustration simmering just below the surface. But she reminded herself that this was Riya's moment of need. We'll see this through, Sandhya promised, her voice resolute, masking the storm within her. Sandhya gave her a ray of hope and said, "Justice will prevail, and I'll help you rebuild, no matter how long it takes."

After enduring weeks of relentless anguish, a fragile light of hope appeared in Riya's gaze. It wasn't much, but it was enough for Sandhya to latch onto. She made a silent promise to stand with her friend and support her as she worked to rebuild what had been lost.

CHAPTER TWO

RESTORING THE SPARK

Next morning, Sandhya barged into Riya's dark lit room, Riya sat sunk in the corner of the couch, gazing at her hands as if her palms subtle soft lines whispered the solutions of her unanswered mysterious questions. Sandhya's heart was filled with sorrow when at the sight of Riya, a shadow of the vibrant, confident young woman she had once been. "Enough, Riya! I told you to stop," Sandhya interrupted, placing a firm hand on her shoulder. "Mukesh can't just escape without consequences. You have every right to justice, and now it's the time to demand it," Sandhya growled, her voice hard with resolved.

Riya's head rose gradually, her expression hollow, stripped of emotion. The light that once sparkled in her eyes was gone, replaced by a shadowy emptiness. "Justice?" she whispered, a faint, enigmatic smile playing on her lips and added, "What's the point, Sandhya? Who cares about justice anymore? Sandhya, Justice is just an illusion. When you look at me, all you see is a spectacle, don't you?"

Riya, please stop it!" Sandhya's voice, thick with emotion, carried both a plea and a command. "You can't let him win by losing yourself. Hold on to your identity it's yours, not his to take." Riya remained frozen, her eyes lingering on the broken tiles below. Sandhya felt helpless, unable to find a way forward. How could she rescue her friend from the shadows when she was already consumed by them herself?

Sandhya inhaled deeply, lowering herself to Riya's level and catching her gaze. "Riya, listen to me," she began, her voice subdued but steadfast. "You're still You, the Riya who filled every room with her spark, the Riya who tackled challenges fearlessly. That person is still within you, and I won't let her be lost."

For the first time, there was a glint in Riya's eyes, a faint shimmer of hope or a tiny echo of her former fiery self. She met Sandhya's firm gaze and saw no hint of pity, only a deep, unwavering conviction. Her fingers shook as she reached for the modest makeup pouch on the table. Sandhya looked on, bewildered, as Riya pulled out a shattered lipstick. With a quiet intensity, she began painstakingly attempting to restore it.

Sandhya frowned in confusion, but then the truth hit her. This wasn't simply an attempt to fix a lipstick, it was a reflection of Riya's struggle to pierce herself back together. With a sharp exhale, Riya's hold on the lipstick tightened. "I can handle this," she said softly, her voice steadying as determination took hold, 'I will handle this.'

Sandhya felt a surge of relief and pride. "That's the Riya I know!", she said, smiling through misty eyes. Riya paused before heading out, her hand closing around the lipstick again. She moved to the uneven mirror coated in dust and, with confident swipes, emblazoned the word *'JUSTICE'* across its surface.

She stared at her reflection, her half-burnt face framed by defiance, and whispered to herself, "It's time!" As they stepped out of the house, Riya waved down a rickshaw. The driver paused briefly his gaze fixed on the scars etched across her skin. He didn't utter a word, but the look alone was enough to shake the fragile confidence she had just begun to rebuild. Hastily, she drew her shawl over her face, concealing the visible reminders of her pain.

Inside the rickshaw, her eyes began to sting with unshed tears, but she forced them back. She wouldn't allow anyone to witness her vulnerability. Not now. When they arrived at the university gate, the watchman peered at her suspiciously. "Your ID Card!" he demanded his tone curt.

Riya handed it over, but his eyes darted between her photograph and her face, his brows furrowing in confusion. "This doesn't look like You.", he said bluntly. "It's me!", Riya replied, her voice breaking slightly.

The watchman hesitated clearly unsure. Sandhya stepped forward her tone sharp and said, "She's a student here! Just let her in." After a tense moment, the watchman relented but insisted on giving Riya a visitor's pass. The humiliation stung, but Riya swallowed her pride and took the pass without a word.

As they walked through the sprawling campus, Riya felt the weight of countless eyes on her. Whispers followed her like shadows.

"Is that her?"

"What happened to her face?"

"She looks so different."

Riya quickened her pace, her limp more pronounced under the strain of their stares. Sandhya stayed close, her hand brushing Riya's arm as a silent gesture of support. They headed straight to the Chemistry lab, where Mukesh was lounging against a desk, laughing loudly as he was flirting with another girl. The sight stopped Riya in her tracks. Her blood ran cold, then boiled with rage.

How could he stand there so carefree, as if he hadn't ruined her life? Her fists clenched, and for a moment, she considered confronting him right then and there. But Sandhya placed a calming hand on her shoulder. "Not here!", she murmured, "Let's go to the Principal first." In the Principal's office, Riya poured out her story, her voice trembling with emotion. Sandhya filled in the gaps, her words sharp and passionate. The Principal listened, her expression shifting from shock to sympathy. "This is unacceptable," the Principal said, her tone grave. "But..." The pause was heavy with unspoken complications. "But what?" Riya demanded. The Principal sighed, "Mukesh's father is a very influential man. He's a major donor to the university. Taking action against his son could have... serious consequences for us."

Riya stared at her disbelief etched across her face, "So you're saying his status is more important than justice even than my life?" The Principal looked away, unable to meet Riya's gaze. "This incident didn't occur on campus. That limits our jurisdiction. I'm very sorry, but my hands are tied." Riya's voice broke as she asked, "Where is humanity? Why is it always that the victim, who has to fight alone?" Sandhya reached for her hand, but Riya pulled away, standing up abruptly. "Thank you for your time, ma'am," she said, her tone icy.

Outside, Riya turned to Sandhya, her eyes brimming with tears, "Is this what justice looks like? Silence? Inaction? How can they all just... look away?" Sandhya didn't know how to answer. Her own heart felt heavy with guilt and helplessness. For a moment, they stood there, the world around them bustling with activity that seemed indifferent to their pain. But then Riya straightened her spine.

"Giving up isn't an option." she said with determination. "If no one will have my back, I'll have my own." Sandhya smiled faintly her hope rekindled. "That's my girl!" she whispered. Hand-in-hand, they moved forward, prepared to confront the unknown.

CHAPTER THREE

SILENT FURY

Riya sat in the shadowy silence of her room her eyes fixed on the cracks running across the wall. Inside the storm of rage and fury churned relentlessly. Her anger clawed at her, pushing her to the edge. Her hands balled into tight fists, her nails biting into her skin, her eyes brimmed with helplessness and anger, on the verge of flowing. The long, sleepless night stretched on, her mind overwhelmed with sorrow and simmering anger.

By morning, she had steeled herself. Together with her friend Sandhya, Riya headed to the local police station. The building stood ahead, its worn exterior showing signs of age with peeling paint and rusted iron grills. A few faded posters hung loosely on the walls, their messages of justice and integrity now seeming out of place in the neglected surroundings. As they stepped inside, the air was filled with the musty scent of damp paper and the faint odour of stale cigarettes, a reminder of the wear and tear the place had endured over the years.

The station was alive with activity, but there was no sense of direction. A constable, his uniform untidy, slouched on a squeaky chair near the door, sipping tea . Papers were scattered carelessly across desks, some teetering on the verge of falling. The atmosphere felt heavy with apathy. As Riya walked in, she could feel the weight of every cold, judgmental gaze upon her, her arrival breaking the monotony of their sluggish routine.

When Riya approached the inspector, a man in his late forties with a thick moustache that curled upward at the edges, he didn't bother looking up from the newspaper he was leisurely flipping through. His shirt strained against his bulky frame, the badge on his chest catching the dull light of the room. The faint scent of cheap cologne wafted from him, mingling unpleasantly with the musty air.

"I need to have a word with you, Sir," Riya said. Her voice faltering as she fought against both anger and fear. The inspector's eyes finally met hers, sweeping over her with a condescending smirk. He didn't bother offering a seat. Instead, he leaned back in his squeaky chair, crossing his arms as if to make it clear that her time was of no value to him.

Noticing her friend's unease, Sandhya moved closer. "Inspector! is this how you treat someone who's come for justice?" she asked in her voice cutting and firm. The inspector's lips curled into a condescending smile, and he motioned lazily to a wooden bench. "Sit, if you want. But make it quick. I don't have all day," he said, his voice dripping with mockery.

Riya sat down, her body tense with humiliation, while Sandhya began narrating the incident. But the inspector seemed uninterested. He tapped his pen rhythmically against the desk, his eyes wandering lazily to the clock on the wall. The other officers in the room exchanged smirks, their disdain palpable.

As Sandhya pressed for an FIR against Mukesh, the inspector's expression soured. He leaned forward, his voice dripping with coldness. "Do you have evidence? If not, don't waste my time."

Riya felt the walls closing in. Her anger bubbled over, but her voice came out in a choked whisper. "How can we get evidence when no one is helping us?" The inspector leaned back with an exaggerated sigh, his smirk returning. "That's your problem, not mine." Riya had reached her limit. She stood up suddenly, her eyes on the verge of tears. Sandhya, furious yet determined to defuse the situation, took hold of Riya's arm and guided her outside. As they left, Riya stole a glance at the inspector's face. His sly grin and the sparkle in his eyes told her he already knew everything about the case. At home, the silence hung heavily in the air. Riya's mother sat quietly in the corner of the living room, her face pale and weary. The light in her eyes, once full of life, had faded. She hadn't said much since everything started, but the grief on her face told a story of its own.

Later that evening, as Riya stepped into her home she felt something cold and sticky on her leg. When she looked down, she saw a thin trickle of blood creeping out from beneath her mother's bedroom door. Her heart froze. A wave of terror washed over her as she hurried toward the door, pounding desperately with her trembling fists.

"Ma! Open the door!", she screamed, but there was no response. Panic flooded her senses. Sandhya, hearing the noise, rushed over and immediately called for help. Within seconds, the neighbours arrived, and they all worked together to break down the door. The scene inside was a nightmare. Blood was everywhere pooling on the floor, staining the walls, soaking into the bed. In the middle of it all lay Riya's mother, lifeless and drenched in red. Her once-gentle hands now cold and motionless.

Riya crumpled to the ground, a piercing scream ripping through the silence. Sandhya knelt down, wrapping an arm around her to steady her trembling form. Amidst the turmoil, Riya's gaze locked onto something that scrawled on the floor in blood, a phone number....

With shaking hands, she dialled the number. The line connected, and a chilling laughter echoed through the receiver. "Hello, Riya," a deep, gravelly voice greeted her. "Looking for justice, are you?"

"Who are you? What do you want?" Riya cried, her voice cracking.

The voice on the other end let out a low, sinister laugh. "I'm the man who killed your mother. And if you continue your little crusade for justice, your father will be next." Riya felt ice in her veins. "Don't hurt him, please", she whispered desperately. "I'll do anything you ask. The murderer's voice turned venomous. "Abandon this fight. Forget Mukesh and your so-called justice. Cross me, and you'll suffer the consequences."

Riya's fingers trembled as she gripped the phone tightly. "I swear, I'll do as you say. Just don't hurt him," she murmured, tears spilling down her cheeks. The call ended, but the ominous words lingered like a shadow over the room. The silence that followed was deafening, but the weight of the threat hung in the air like a noose. Riya sank to the floor, her body convulsing with sobs. Sandhya wrapped her arms around her, but no words of comfort could mend what was broken. The room, once a sanctuary of love and warmth, was now a crime scene drenched in despair. And somewhere out there, the man who had stolen everything from Riya walked free and untouched, his authority rooted in fear and corruption that shielded him.

CHAPTER FOUR

TEARS OF VENGEANCE

Riya sat frozen next to her mother's still body, the air thick with grief and an eerie quietness. Her mother's pale face, streaked with blood, was a chilling sight that held Riya's gaze captive. She felt paralyzed, her heart silently roaring with pain. The world dissolved into a haze as tears streamed down her face, dripping softly onto the cold, lifeless hand she clung to, unwilling to let go.

Suddenly, a group of officials entered, their grim faces matching the mood of the room. One of them, a middle-aged man with a stern demeanour and a badge pinned to his chest, cleared his throat. "We need to take the body for post-mortem.", he said gently but firmly. Riya held onto her mother's hand as though letting go, would shatter her entirely. "No, please!", she stammered, her voice barely a whisper, cracking under the weight of her anguish.

"Miss, we understand this is difficult.", the official continued as his tone was softening. "But this is necessary to investigate what happened. Please cooperate." Sandhya, sensing Riya's inability to respond, knelt beside her. "Riya, they need to do this. It's the only way to find justice for your mom", she said, her voice trembling but resolute.

Riya didn't reply. She sat frozen, her gaze fixed on her mother's serene yet lifeless face. Sandhya exchanged a glance with the officials, nodding for them to proceed. With careful hands, they wrapped the body in a white sheet and prepared to take it away. Before leaving, one of the officers turned to Riya. "Do you suspect anyone?" he asked, his pen hovering over a notepad. Riya hesitated. The murderer's words echoed in her mind: If you seek justice, your father will die. Though the truth burnt inside her, she remained silent. Her lips trembled, but no words escaped them. The officer sighed and left with the others, leaving the room heavy with grief.

As the body was carried out, Riya's father stood in the corner, his face ashen. Tears streamed down his cheeks, and his body trembled as he watched his wife being taken away. "How... how did this happen?", he mumbled. His voice barely audible. His eyes, red and swollen looked hollow. He turned away, unable to bear the sight. Riya's grandparents arrived soon after, their faces etched with worry and sorrow. They bombarded her with questions, their voices rising in panic. "Riya, what happened? Who would do such a thing?" her grandmother cried, clutching her chest as if the weight of the tragedy would crush her.

But Riya remained silent. She couldn't muster the strength to explain, to relive the nightmare. Sandhya stepped in, trying her best to manage the situation. "She needs time," Sandy said firmly, placing a protective arm around Riya. The entire house was enveloped in mourning. When the officials returned her mother's body, now wrapped entirely in a pristine white cloth, Riya broke down. She fell to her knees beside her mother, sobbing uncontrollably. The sight of her mother, once so full of life, now cold and unmoving, shattered her completely.

She clutched her mother's feet, pressing her forehead against them as her tears soaked the white cloth. "I'm sorry, Ma," she whispered, her voice trembling. "I'm so, so sorry." Her cries echoed through the house, and no words of comfort from those around her could reach her. Riya's mind was a whirlwind of guilt and grief. She blamed herself for her mother's death, replaying the murderer's threats over and over.

Amidst her tears, she began to speak softly, as if her mother could still hear her. "Ma, you were my anchor, my guiding light. Every step I took, you were there, holding my hand, steadying me. When I fell, you picked me up. When I strayed, you set me right. You stayed awake all night when I was sick, singing softly to calm me. When you scolded me, it was only to make me better. And the very next moment, you'd pull me into your arms, your love wrapping around me like a warm blanket. Because of you, Ma, I cleared NEET. It was your belief in me that brought me here, to this medical college. But now... now you're gone. How am I supposed to move on without you?"

Riya's voice cracked, and tears spilled onto her mother's body as she recited a poem she'd written in that moment of raw emotion:

"Oh, Ma, your hands held my first steps so tight,
You shielded me in darkness, your love my light.
Every tear you wiped, every fear you stilled,
With you, my heart, my world, was filled.
Now you lie silent, my words meet air,
The warmth of your hug, I seek, despair.
But in my heart, your love will stay,
Guiding my steps, come what may."

As the final lines left her lips, Riya collapsed into sobs, burying her face in her mother's lap.

In the crowd gathered outside, a figure stood apart. He was a tall man with sharp features, his dark eyes cold and calculating. A faint, almost imperceptible smile played on his lips as he watched Riya's anguish. It sent a shiver down her spine when their eyes met.

Something about him felt wrong, terribly wrong. Her heart raced, and a surge of determination washed over her. She quickly pulled out her phone and dialled the number she'd found that was written in blood. But this time, the phone didn't ring. Her suspicion deepened, and she turned to Sandy. "That man....", she whispered, pointing discreetly. "I'm sure he's involved. It's him... it's him, I know it."

Sandhya nodded cautiously. "We'll figure this out. But for now, Riya, you need to stay strong." Riya's tears flowed relentlessly as memories of her mother flooded her mind. She recalled how her mother's hands steadied her first wobbly steps, how she stayed up all night when Riya had fever, how she corrected her mistakes with love and patience.

Turning to her father, she took his trembling hands in hers. "Papa, I promise you," she said, her voice steady despite the tears streaming down her face. "No matter what happens, I'll never leave you. I'll take care of you. We'll get through this together."

Her father nodded, his eyes brimming with tears as he held her tightly. The house was filled with sorrow, the air heavy with grief, but amidst it all, Riya made a silent vow, she would seek justice for her mother. She would fight back, no matter the cost.

CHAPTER FIVE

STORM OF GRIEF

The day of Riya's mother's funeral, dawned heavy with sorrow, the skies mirroring the grief that engulfed everyone. Dark, menacing clouds loomed overhead, and torrential rain fell relentlessly, as if the heavens mourned alongside the family. The sound of the downpour mixed with the low murmurs of the gathered mourners, creating an almost oppressive atmosphere.

Inside the dimly lit room, the air was thick with the fragrance of incense and the salty tang of tears. Riya stood near her mother's casket, her face pale and streaked with tears. Her heart felt like it was being crushed under an unbearable weight. The priest began the sacred chants, the rhythmic recitations blending with the steady drumming of rain against the windows.

As the rituals proceeded, Riya struggled to maintain her composure. The sight of her mother, her face serene yet lifeless, surrounded by garlands of jasmine and marigold, brought her to the brink of collapse. Her breathing grew shallow, her chest tight. She clutched her head, swaying slightly as her vision blurred.

Suddenly, Riya gasped and fell to the ground with a thud, her body convulsing violently. Her eyes rolled back, revealing only the whites, and her limbs twitched uncontrollably. Foam gathered at the corners of her lips as she struggled for breath. A collective gasp erupted from the mourners, and chaos ensued.

"Help her!" her father screamed, rushing to her side. A few men carefully turned her onto her side to prevent choking while others frantically called for an ambulance. Her breathing was shallow, her body trembling as the seizure gripped her mercilessly. Outside, the rain seemed to grow heavier, the storm mirroring the panic inside.

When the ambulance arrived, paramedics quickly assessed her condition, stabilizing her as best they could before whisking her away to the hospital. Riya's father, torn between his unconscious daughter and the funeral rites, made the painful decision to stay and complete the ceremonies.

At the cremation ground, the rain drenched everyone as they followed the priest's instructions. Umbrellas did little to shield them from the deluge as they watched the casket being placed for the final rites. The sacred fire hissed and sputtered under the relentless rain, but the rituals continued. Smoke mixed with the misty rain, creating a hauntingly ethereal scene. As the flames consumed the casket, the mourners bowed their heads in silent prayer, bidding a tearful farewell.

Hours later, Riya awoke in a sterile hospital room, her body weak and her mind foggy. The doctor advised rest, but her heart yearned to see her mother one last time. By the time she was discharged, the funeral was over, leaving her with a deep sense of regret and despair.

With trembling steps, Riya walked to her mother's graveyard, the rain still falling in a soft drizzle. Her father held an umbrella over her, but she didn't care about the rain soaking her clothes. Her eyes were fixed on the fresh mound of earth, adorned with garlands and petals. Kneeling beside the grave, she picked up a handful of the flowers, her tears mixing with the rain as they fell onto the petals.

"I'm so sorry, Ma," she whispered, her voice barely audible over the sound of the rain. "I couldn't even say goodbye." Her father knelt beside her, pulling her into a tight embrace. They held each other, their sobs the only sound cutting through the steady patter of rain. The world around them seemed to blur, their shared grief the only thing anchoring them in that moment.

As Riya looked up, her tear-filled eyes caught a figure in the distance. Mukesh stood under a tree, the shadowy outlines of his face barely visible through the mist and rain. To her shock, he was smiling at her a chilling, misplaced expression that sent shivers down her spine. "Why...?" she whispered, rising to her feet. She tried to approach him, her steps unsteady on the rain-soaked ground. But as she neared, Mukesh turned and disappeared into the mist. Her heart pounded with a mix of fear and confusion. The unsettling image of his smile stayed with her as she returned to her father's side.

Drained of energy and spirit, Riya returned home with her father. The house felt emptier than ever, every corner a painful reminder of her mother's absence. The rain continued to fall outside, its sound now a sober backdrop to their shared silence. Riya sat in the living room, clutching her mother's favourite scarf, inhaling the faint scent of her mother that still lingered on it.

Her father placed a hand on hers, his grip firm yet comforting. "We'll get through this," he said softly, his voice trembling with unspoken pain. But for Riya, the weight of the day felt insurmountable. The rain outside mirrored the storm within her, a torrent of grief and unanswered questions that would take a lifetime to quell.

21

CHAPTER SIX

BEYOND THE STORM

The next day, Riya sat quietly in her shadowed room, the depth of her despair wrapping around her like a dense fog. Outside, the weather matched her despair; the rain hammered the windows in a wild frenzy, and the wind screamed through the streets, unsettling everything it touched. The urgent tone of the news anchor drifted in from the adjacent room. In the living room, Riya's father sat, his face drained of colour as he watched the storm's progress. The storm over the ocean had quickly transformed into a raging cyclone, charging toward their region with ferocity. The anchor's alerts about safety protocols barely registered, as Riya remained engulfed in her personal turmoil.

She lay still on the cold floor, her vacant eyes fixed on the ceiling as her mind churned with a storm of anguish and sorrow. Every memory of her mother felt like a fresh wound, each one cutting deeper than the last. The rhythmic drumming of the rain against the roof provided a bleak soundtrack to her grief, amplifying the emptiness within her.

As her gaze drifted across the room, it stopped on a mirror resting against the wall. The reflective glass revealed a glimpse of the curtains her mother had tenderly crafted just a short while ago. Riya's gaze fixed on them, her heart tightening as she noticed the intricate details. The curtains were adorned with a half-burnt heart a design her mother had stitched recently. A golden sun, its rays shimmering in intricate threads, stretched above the heart, casting light across the dark fabric.

For a moment, Riya was puzzled by the design, but then, as though a light had pierced through her fog of grief, the meaning became clear. Her mother had always believed in resilience, in finding hope even in the darkest of times. The sun was her mother's silent message, a reminder that no matter how charred or broken the heart might feel, there was always hope to guide it.

Something inside Riya sparked with the realization. She sat up, her tears falling faster, no longer in sorrow but with a newfound resolve. Her mother had always wanted Riya to fight for justice, for truth, and for a better world. The sun, defiantly shining on the curtain, was her mother's final gift, a silent call to rise above the pain.

Fuelled by her newfound determination, Riya got to her feet and headed to the storeroom. Her hands fumbled through the dusty shelves until she found the photo albums, stacked neatly in a corner. She carried them back to her room and sat cross-legged on the floor, the storm outside raging on as if to match the storm of emotions within her.

As Riya flipped open the first album, her eyes locked onto a picture of her mother, gently holding her tiny hands as she took her first steps. The pride in her mother's smile was undeniable. Riya's heart squeezed as she traced the edges of the photo, whispering, "You never gave up on me, Ma. I won't give up now, I promise."

As she turned each page, memories came flooding back. There was a picture from her first birthday, her mother holding her tenderly as she reached for the cake. Another image showed them laughing together in the park, her mother's joy captured forever in the photograph.

Then, there were the photos from their family vacations. One that stood out was from a trip to Goa when Riya was only five. She remembered losing herself in the colourful shells and the sound of the waves on the crowded beach. Her mother's desperate cries still echoed in her mind as she recalled being found after what felt like forever. Her mother had collapsed to her knees, holding her tightly, tears flowing as she scolded and comforted her in the same breath

The album was a reminder of her mother's unshakeable love, her inner strength, and the sacrifices that went unnoticed. One photo showed them under the blooming cherry blossoms, her mother's arm protectively around her. Another captured her mother braiding her hair, her face serene and focused on the task.

Each photo was a tribute to the way her mother had shaped her into who she was. Though the storm outside grew more intense, Riya felt a sense of calm strength rising within her. Her grief remained, but it no longer crippled her. Instead, it fuelled her, becoming a fire that urged her to honour her mother's memory by living the life her mother had always wished for her.

Closing the album, Riya sat in silence for a moment, the sound of the rain like a heartbeat in the background. She glanced back at the curtain, the golden sun now glowing faintly in the dim light. "I promise, I'll make you proud,

Ma!", she murmured. Her voice calm and determined. The storm continued to rage outside, but within her, a calm determination had taken root. It was time to act, to step out of the shadows of despair and into the light her mother had always envisioned for her.

CHAPTER SEVEN

WHERE SHADOWS SPEAK

The house was unnervingly quiet as Riya drifted from room to room, her thoughts tangled and unspoken. But when her gaze fell on her father in the living room, everything seemed to freeze. His eyes were bloodshot, and his face was pale, drained of life. He sat motionless, his gaze lost in the rain-drenched window, as though he were looking for something maybe peace, maybe answers, or perhaps both though the emptiness in his stare made it clear that nothing could be found.

Riya approached him slowly, her voice tender yet determined. "Dad, you haven't eaten all day. It's almost night. Please, eat something. For me?" Her father turned to her slowly, his gaze heavy with sadness. "Riya," he began, his voice trembling, "Life without your mother... it's not easy. If I even skipped a meal, her heart would beat so hard. She would never let me stay hungry. And now... who will take care of me?" His voice cracked as tears welled in his eyes. "I have only you left, Riya. Please, I beg you, don't abandon me when I grow old. That's my only request."

Riya felt a pang deep in her chest. She sank to her knees beside him, her hand wrapping around his with a desperation that matched his own. Tears streamed down her face as she spoke, her voice trembling with emotion. "Papa, please, don't say that. It breaks me to hear you like this. No matter what comes, I will never leave you. I promise, I'll always be here for you, always."

Her father pulled her into a tight embrace, his sobs muffled against her shoulder. For a long moment, they held each other, united in their grief and their determination to move forward. Determined to comfort him, Riya stood up and headed to the kitchen. She wasn't a great cook, but she decided to make dosas for her father. Her hands shook as she mixed the batter, and the results were far from perfect. The dosas turned out to be hard and uneven, but she carried them to her father with a smile.

"Papa, I made this for you," she said, holding out the plate with a nervous smile. "I know it's far from perfect, but..." Her father took a bite, chewing slowly as he considered the taste. Despite the unevenness, he managed a gentle smile. Riya carefully fed her father, her hands steady despite the weight of the moment. "We'll get through this, Papa," she said softly. "I'll take care of you, and together, we'll fight for justice. Mom would want us to do this."

That night, Riya mapped out their next steps. She knew she would need allies, resources, and, most importantly, courage. But when she reached out to Sandhya, a close friend she had counted on, her hopes quickly crumbled. Sandhya's voice was cold, her tone sharp as she declined to help. Riya felt a sharp pang in her chest, confusion and hurt swirling in her mind. What had happened? Why had Sandhya abandoned her when she needed her most?

Her father suggested seeking the help of Lawyer Rakesh, a family acquaintance known for his strong sense of justice. Although Riya understood the risks of this journey, particularly for her father, she couldn't allow fear to hold her back. The memory of her mother, along with the sun stitched into the curtain, fuelled her determination to keep moving forward.

That night, as Riya lay in bed, an unsettling sensation crept over her. The room felt suffocating, as though an invisible presence hovered in the air. Her heart pounded, but she pressed her palms together and whispered mantras, seeking comfort and protection. Gradually, the eerie feeling lifted, and she eventually succumbed to a restless, uneasy sleep. The next morning Riya and her father made their way to Lawyer Rakesh's office.

The lawyer's office felt like a world apart from the tempest raging outside. It was spacious yet cluttered, with a single overhead lamp casting a soft, amber glow over the chaos of papers strewn across the desk. The piles of legal documents seemed ready to collapse at any moment, each stack a silent testament to years of hard work. The walls were lined with shelves, sagging under the weight of well-worn, leather-bound law books, their spines creased from years of use. A faded map of the city hung on one wall, and on the other, certificates and accolades framed in gold gleamed proudly, reflecting Rakesh's deep expertise and dedication.

In the centre of the room sat Lawyer Rakesh himself. He was an imposing figure tall and broad-shouldered, with a presence that commanded attention. His neatly combed hair was peppered with grey, and his square jaw was set in a firm line. He wore a crisp white shirt rolled up at the sleeves, revealing strong, veined arms. His sharp eyes, framed by thin glasses, scanned a document with intense focus.

When Riya and her father walked in, Rakesh looked up, his expression softening just a bit. Rising from his chair, he extended a hand to her father. His voice, deep and calm, held a note of sincerity. "It's good to see you both," he said. "I've heard about your loss. Please accept my deepest condolences.

Riya studied the man carefully. His presence exuded confidence, and she sensed that he was someone who could truly help them. "We need your help, Rakesh Ji," her father said, his voice trembling. "We want justice for my wife and daughter. Rakesh nodded thoughtfully, motioning for them to sit. "Go ahead and tell me everything," he said, his voice calm but resolute

As Riya and her father unfolded their story, the storm outside raged on, but within the lawyer's office, a different kind of storm was brewing a storm of determination and the pursuit of justice.

CHAPTER EIGHT

UNMASKED

The storm outside raged on, its fury tapping against the windows, but inside Riya's chest, the storm was more personal, a maelstrom of grief and determination. She sat across from Lawyer Rakesh, her fingers fidgeting with the hem of her sleeve as she gathered the strength to speak. The room, cluttered with papers and the musty scent of old leather, felt heavy with expectation. Rakesh, however, remained calm, his sharp eyes never leaving hers. He leaned forward slightly, his presence grounding her as she began to tell their story. At first, her words came in shaky bursts, her voice a fragile whisper, but with each passing moment, she grew steadier, more resolute no longer just recounting the past but preparing to fight for the future.

When she finished, the silence that followed was profound, broken only by the faint rhythm of the rain outside. Rakesh reclined slightly in his chair, his face a blend of contemplation and resolve. "Riya," he began, his tone unwavering, "this journey won't be an easy one. But let me assure you, we will leave no stone unturned in our pursuit of justice. By coming forward and sharing your story, you've already demonstrated incredible courage."

His words felt like a balm to her frayed nerves, reigniting a flicker of hope. Then, leaning forward, his hands clasped, he asked, "Do you have any suspicions? Is there someone you think might be behind this?"

Riya's eyes burned with an intensity that matched the storm outside. Her fist struck the table with a resounding thud, scattering papers like fallen leaves. "It's Mukesh!" she spat, her voice trembling with rage. "I know it's him I'd stake everything on it!"

Rakesh raised a brow, his sharp gaze narrowing. "That's a strong accusation. Do you have any evidence to support it?"

For a moment, Riya froze. The fire in her eyes dimmed, replaced by a flicker of uncertainty. She stared at her hands, her mind racing, but she came up empty. The room felt suffocating, the air thick with tension. Rakesh noticed her struggle and gestured toward the faint scar on her arm. "What about this?" he asked, his voice probing yet gentle. "It's an undeniable mark. It could be evidence, but the challenge is proving its connection to Mukesh."

Riya looked at her scar as though seeing it for the first time. It had been a silent witness to her pain, a story etched into her skin. But now, it seemed to carry a new weight, a chance for justice "Can we check the CCTV footage from the park?", she asked hesitantly. Her voice tinged with both hope and desperation.

Rakesh nodded slowly, but his brow furrowed. "I'll try," he replied. "But there's a catch. Without filing an FIR, it's difficult to pursue this case officially. And we both know this isn't an ordinary situation. The police may already be compromised. This is no cakewalk, Riya. It's a labyrinth, and every step is fraught with danger.

His words were a stark reminder of the tough road that lay ahead. Yet, as a trusted family friend, he assured them that he would spare no effort in pursuing every lead, beginning with the CCTV footage. "If we manage to secure that," he said, his voice resolute, "It could give us the leverage we need to approach the authorities and officially file an FIR."

Riya's heart swelled with appreciation for the lawyer, his steadfast determination bolstering her own. "I'm counting on you, Rakesh Ji," she said, her voice calmer now, tinged with a newfound confidence. "I have faith in you."

As Riya stepped out of the office, the storm had cleared, leaving behind a soft glow of sunlight streaming through the dissipating clouds. The world around her felt renewed, as if it too had emerged from the chaos. She paused, letting the warmth of the sun wrap around her like a comforting embrace. Tilting her head toward the sky, she let the sunlight wash over her, and for the first time over many days, a smile broke through, a glimmer of hope in the air.

As Riya looked up at the sky, now clear and calm with soft blues and whites, she felt a quiet sense of relief. The storm, both outside and within, had passed. The harsh winds and rain had faded, leaving behind a stillness that seemed to reflect her own thoughts. She knew the road ahead wouldn't be easy, but for the first time in days, she felt a small sense of peace, as if she had taken the first step towards something better.

Her lips curled into a determined smile, her eyes glinting with newfound purpose. "Mukesh," she whispered under her breath, her voice resolute, "Your time is coming. Justice will find you."

As Riya gazed at the sky, now calm and bathed in gentle hues of blue and white, a wave of quiet relief washed over her. The storm, both outside and within, had finally begun to subside. The fierce winds and relentless rain were gone, leaving a tranquil silence that mirrored her shifting thoughts. Though she knew the path ahead would be far from simple, for the first time in days, she felt a glimmer of peace, as if the hardest part was behind her and she was now stepping into something more hopeful.

CHAPTER NINE

NIGHT OF SECRETS

Riya reached home and collapsed onto her bed, overwhelmed by the whirlwind of emotions and unanswered questions. As she picked up her phone, notifications flooded the screen missed calls, messages, and reminders of her mother's absence. The sheer volume was suffocating, each ping a dagger to her fragile heart. She couldn't bear it anymore. "Overcoming with anguish, she flung the phone across the room and dissolved into uncontrollable tears. Her sobs reverberated through the house, prompting her father to rush to her side."

Sundar dashed in, his heart clenching at the sight of his daughter huddled on the floor, her sobs shaking her frail frame. 'Riya,' he said softly, lowering himself beside her, 'Please, don't let this consume you. I'm here.' His words, though tender, did little to ease her torment. Unable to hold back his emotions, Sundar wept as well. Their shared anguish filled the room, an unspoken testament to the depth of their pain."

Sundar's phone buzzed on the table, cutting through the heavy atmosphere. He wiped his cheeks and walked over to check the caller ID. It was Rakesh, their family lawyer. His expression shifted, a faint glimmer of optimism surfacing as he darted toward the phone. But before he could pick it up, the screen went dark. 'Not now, not like this!' Sundar groaned, his hands trembling as he desperately tried to reconnect with Rakesh. Each ring went unanswered, and frustration mounted until, finally a message notification lit up his phone.

The message was brief but devastating:

"I am sorry, Mr. Sundar. I tried my level best, but I am backing out of this case for my family's welfare. I don't want to lose them over this. Please, for your safety and your daughter's, back off too." Sundar's voice broke as he read the message aloud, each syllable laced with pain. The room fell into an unbearable stillness. Riya, her gaze fixed downward, shot to her feet without warning. Her face betrayed no emotion, but her eyes burnt with a fire that needed no words. She stormed out, leaving the door swinging shut behind her.

"Riya!" her father called after her, his voice tinged with panic. "Come back! Where are you going?" But Riya didn't look back. She moved quickly, her feet carrying her without direction. She felt a desperate need to escape, to act, to do something. The streets blurred around her as she walked, her mind a tangled web of grief and determination.

"Rounding the corner, Riya's eyes fell on a familiar face, Sandhya. Her once inseparable friend, striding quickly down the opposite sidewalk. 'Sandhya!' Riya called out, but her voice went unanswered. Instead, Sandhya moved farther away, crossing to the other side. Frustration mounting, Riya sprinted after her, clutching Sandhya's arm with such intensity that she let out a startled gasp. "This only fuelled Riya's desperation. She ran after her, grabbing

Sandhya's arm with such force that the latter gasped."

"Why are you shutting me out?" Riya asked, her voice firm and unwavering. "I need to know!"Sandhya glanced around anxiously, her face ashen and her eyes flickering as if expecting someone to appear. "Let me go, Riya," she murmured, her voice shaky and urgent. "You shouldn't have come here. It's not safe."

Riya's grip only grew firmer, her frustration boiling over. 'Not until you tell me what's happening!' she snapped.

Sandhya sighed, her shoulders sagging in defeat. "Fine," she hissed, her tone barely audible. "Follow me. But don't speak to me, and keep your head down." Riya was surprised by how quickly Sandhya's mood changed. The fear was palpable, but Riya didn't hesitate. She pulled a shawl over her head, obscuring her face as they made their way through the crowded streets. Their pace was purposeful, every backward glance filled with unease.

When they reached Sandhya's home, Riya couldn't help but notice how modest and ran down. The small, single-storey house was tucked into a quiet lane, its peeling paint and rusted iron gate hinting at years of neglect. A dim yellow bulb flickered on the porch, casting long shadows across the cracked tiles.

The air was dense with the scent of aged spices and a damp, earthy smell. The living room was cramped, furnished with an assortment of mismatched items, and the carpet, worn and faded, had long lost its original charm. In one corner, a small altar with flickering candles and a garlanded photograph of a deity provided the only vibrant spot in the room.

Emerging from the kitchen, Sandhya's mother was draped in a timeworn saree, her fragile frame barely visible beneath it. Her face, worn with the passage of time, held kind but tired eyes. She blinked in surprise when she saw Riya but quickly hid her astonishment behind a polite nod. 'Who is this, Sandhya?' she asked softly, her voice laden with exhaustion but gentle in tone. "Just a friend!" Sandhya replied hurriedly, avoiding her mother's gaze. "We need to talk in private."

Without waiting for a response, Sandhya led Riya to her small bedroom at the back of the house. The room was cluttered with books, clothes, and a single cot covered in a faded bedsheet. A small window let in the dim light of the evening, its iron bars adding a sense of confinement.

As soon as they were alone, Sandhya closed the door and turned to Riya, her face a mask of fear and urgency. "Why did you follow me?" she asked, her voice shaking. "You shouldn't have come here!" Sandhya," Riya said, her tone resolute, as she moved nearer, "I understand you're terrified, but if you know anything, no matter how small, you have to share it. My mother deserves justice. Sandhya hesitated for a moment, her eyes filling with tears. The room felt suffocating, the silence thick with the weight of untold secrets. Finally, with a shaky exhale, Sandhya whispered, "There's something you should know, but it's not safe here. You have to leave before it's too late."

CHAPTER TEN

THE WARNING

The faint light in Sandhya's tiny room cast long, haunting shadows, adding to the suffocating silence. Sandhya's eyes brimmed with tears as she leaned in towards Riya, her voice trembling and barely audible. "Riya, it's Mukesh, just like you thought. But there's more to it than you can imagine." Riya leaned forward, her heartbeat quickening, sensing the weight of Sandhya's words. "What do you mean?" she whispered, her voice almost breaking.

"It wasn't only Mukesh," Sandhya continued, her voice soft as a whisper. "His father... his father is tied to your mother's murder." The words hit Riya like a thunderclap. Her knees buckled, and for a moment, the room seemed to tilt. Her thoughts raced, trying to process the revelation, but a surge of anger and despair quickly followed. "How do you know all this?" She pressed, her voice cracking with both disbelief and a desperate need for answers.

Sandhya paused, her fingers shaking as she dug into her pocket and retrieved a wrinkled piece of paper. The letter, creased and worn, seemed to carry a heaviness in its ominous message. She handed it to Riya silently, her eyes pleading for comprehension. Riya's hands shook as she unfolded the letter. The paper was smudged and worn, but the words were chillingly clear. It was addressed to Sandhya and contained a dire warning:

"Sandhya, stay out of this case. If you involve yourself, your mother will be the next target. Do not test us."

Riya gasped as she read the letter, the horrifying implications sinking in. She lifted her gaze to Sandhya, her mind reeling with disbelief. "Why would they send this to you? How are you connected to all of this?"

Sandhya's voice cracked as she began to explain. Her gaze fixed on the floor. "I saw it, Riya." I was there in the park that day. I saw when Mukesh... when he tried to. Her voice faltered, but she forced herself to continue. "When he tried to hurt you, and the acid splashed on your face. I couldn't move. I was terrified. But later, I confronted Mukesh. I threatened to report him to the principal."

Riya's gaze sharpened in shock as Sandhya continued, her tears falling in steady streams. "Your mother was murdered, and that same day, this letter arrived. I was paralyzed with fear, Riya. I didn't know how to protect you or my own mother. Sandhya dropped to her knees her hands clasped together in a desperate plea. "I'm so sorry, Riya. I was a coward. I should have stood by you, but I couldn't risk my mother's life. Please, forgive me."

Riya's face softened despite the storm raging within her. She bent down and held Sandhya's trembling hands her voice steady but filled with pain. "Sandhya, I understand. You were scared, just like anyone would be. You're not to blame for their evil. But I can't stay here. It's not safe for you or your mother if I do." With tears flowing, Sandhya clung to Riya, her sobs uncontrollable. "I'm sorry," she murmured, her voice muffled by Riya's shoulder as she sought comfort.

Riya pulled back slowly her eyes clouded with tears. "Please, take care of yourself, Sandhya, and watch over your mother." As Riya turned to leave, Sandhya's mother appeared at the door, her face lined with worry. "Beta," she said softly, "Have some tea before you go." Riya shook her head, her voice almost inaudible. "Thanks, Aunty, but I have to go." With that, she turned and hurried out, wrapping her scarf more tightly around her face to conceal both her scar and the turmoil within. The crisp evening breeze greeted her as she stepped outside, yet it offered no relief from the storm raging inside her. Her pace quickened as she walked home, her mind cycling through the unsettling truths. When she finally arrived at her doorstep, her father stood there, eyes filled with concern.

"Riya, where were you?" Sundar asked, his voice filled with concern. Riya said nothing in response. She stormed past him, slamming her bedroom door so hard that the mirror on the wall cracked, fragments scattering across the floor. Sundar knocked urgently, his voice pleading. "Riya, open the door! Please, just talk to me!

Inside, Riya sank to the floor, leaning against the door as she buried her face in her hands. The weight of the day was unbearable, and she sobbed uncontrollably. A sharp migraine pulsed in her head, the physical pain intensifying her emotional torment.

At last, exhaustion overcame her, and she drifted into a restless sleep on the cold floor, her tears still damp on her cheeks.

CHAPTER ELEVEN

PAGES OF PAIN

The room was filled with an unsettling quiet when Riya suddenly woke, her breath quick and her heart racing. The nightmare lingered in her mind like a heavy fog, refusing to fade. In her dream, she had been transported to the first day she met Mukesh in the college cafeteria. She could almost taste the coffee she had been drinking, hear the soft buzz of conversations around her, and feel the sharpness of his gaze as they exchanged their first words. The memory in her nightmare felt so vivid, so alive, that she woke with a sharp shriek, clutching her bedsheet as though it could shield her from the haunting visions.

Her eyes, wide with fear, flicked around the room until they settled on the comforting familiarity of her surroundings. "It's just a dream," She murmured, her voice shaky. She attempted to calm her breathing, but her heart continued to pound relentlessly in her chest.

The ticking of the clock on her wall echoed loudly in the stillness, each tick amplifying the passage of time into an endless stretch. She glanced at the glowing numbers at 2:00 AM. Sleep remained elusive, and she tossed and turned, her mind spinning with disjointed, haunting thoughts. When fatigue finally pulled her into slumber, it offered no relief.

This time, her dream hurled her back to the park, to that nightmarish day. She could feel the scalding burn of the acid on her skin, the suffocating terror in her chest as Mukesh's menacing grin drew nearer. The dream jolted her awake again, and this time, she broke down, her body wracked with uncontrollable sobs of anguish and fear. Her unsteady hands fumbled for her diary on the bedside table. She wrote feverishly, spilling every fragment of the nightmare onto the pages as though trapping it in ink could keep it from haunting her any longer.

After whispering a quiet prayer, hoping for solace and strength, Riya lay down again. The night eventually loosened its grip, and she slipped into a deep, dreamless sleep. Yet, when she awoke at 10:00 AM, the exhaustion was undeniable. Her head ached, and her limbs felt leaden, as though the night had drained every bit of her energy.

She dragged herself to the bathroom, her steps sluggish and reluctant. The fragmented images of her nightmares clung to her consciousness like cobwebs, stubborn and inescapable. As she stood under the shower, hoping the cold water would jolt her awake, her father's voice broke through her haze. "Riya, breakfast is ready. Please eat something," Sundar called, his tone laced with concern.

Riya eased the door open, her weary eyes meeting his anxious gaze. He had tried everything to lift her spirits, and today, he had prepared upma the one dish she disliked. Still, she dragged herself to the table, mustering a faint smile as she began eating. The sticky texture was unappealing, but she forced it down, unwilling to let her father see her disappointment

After breakfast, Riya felt compelled to pick up her diary. As she leafed through its pages, a subtle sense of discomfort crept over her, a quiet murmur in her mind warning that something was off. Her gaze settled on her mother's photograph, and she gently ran her fingers over the frame. A renewed wave of sorrow engulfed her, and tears began to flow uncontrollably.

Soon, her uncle Rajan arrived, bringing a soothing presence to the somber atmosphere. Though his eyes reflected his own grief, his resolve to cheer Riya up was clear. "Come, Riya. Let's take a walk," he urged softly.

"I don't feel like it, Uncle," she replied, her voice barely above a whisper. He crouched beside her, placing a comforting hand on her shoulder. "I promise, you'll be glad you came. Trust me." With hesitation, Riya agreed, and they headed down the lively street. The fresh air carried subtle hints of blooming flowers and warm, freshly baked bread. The road was flanked by shops, their vibrant displays of clothes, trinkets, and sweets drawing the attention of pedestrians. Street vendors called out enthusiastically, their voices weaving a cheerful melody into the morning hustle.

Rajan brought Riya to a charming bookstore tucked away in a serene corner of the street. The shelves were packed with books, their worn spines telling stories of countless readers who had cherished them. "I thought this place might brighten your mood,", he said softly, offering a kind smile. Riya's fingers glided over the books absentmindedly, silently appreciating his gesture, though the heaviness in her heart lingered.

They paused at a small chai stall, where the rich aroma of spiced tea lingered in the air. Rajan handed her a hot cup, and they sipped in tranquil silence. The heat of the tea seeped into her, and for a brief moment, a hint of serenity settled over her.

As they walked further, they passed a toy shop, its window filled with stuffed animals and vibrant toys. A group of children giggled as they played nearby, their laughter like a balm to Riya's aching soul.

Finally, Rajan bought two plates of steaming hot samosas from a street vendor. "Come on, Riya. I know you can't resist these," he teased, his tone light-hearted. Riya managed a faint smile and took a bite. The crispy shell and spicy filling brought a sliver of comfort.

As they walked back home, Riya felt a tiny spark of hope reignite within her. Rajan's efforts to distract her, to remind her of the small joys in life, hadn't erased her pain, but they had eased it, if only for a moment. When they reached the house, she hugged him tightly, whispering, "Thank you, Uncle."

Rajan smiled and patted her head. "One step at a time, Riya. You'll get through this. I know you will."

CHAPTER TWELVE

THE WAKE UP CALL

Riya sat at her desk her journal open before her. The weight of the day pressed down like a storm cloud, but her determination burnt bright. She poured her thoughts onto the page, intent on preserving the memories while they were vivid. Her hand shook faintly as she wrote, "Her death will not be meaningless. Justice will be served."

The conversations with her Uncle Rajan lingered in her mind, replaying like scenes from a nostalgic home video. The bookstore, the chai stall, the crisp samosa it all felt surreal now, like fleeting snapshots of a life she couldn't fully grasp. One memory stood out more clearly than the others. At the bookstore, she had chosen a copy of 'The Interpretation of Dreams by Sigmund Freud'. The title struck a deep chord within her, its exploration of dreams and their meanings aligning with her recent reflections. That evening, after dinner, she opened her laptop and delved into researching the book. Her fingers moved swiftly over the keyboard as she uncovered its core concept: how dreams often expose glimpses of hidden desires, buried fears, or unresolved conflicts from real life.

Riya reclined in her chair, her thoughts spinning wildly. Is this a sign? she pondered. Her own dreams felt strikingly similar vivid, haunting, and inexplicably intertwined with the turmoil she was facing. Exhausted but restless, Riya crawled into bed. The silence of the night was oppressive, wrapping around her like a heavy blanket. As she drifted off, the boundary between dreams and reality began to blur once again.

A strange sensation crept over Riya before she could make sense of it. Her bed seemed alive beneath her, shifting and tugging, as if the mattress itself were dissolving into quicksand. Her chest tightened as her breathing grew rapid, each gasp laced with growing dread. Summoning the courage to open her eyes, she was met with a sight that made her blood run cold, rooting her to the spot.

Across the room, partially hidden by the dim lighting, was Mukesh, his presence both haunting and undeniable. Her heart hammered in her chest, each beat echoing through her trembling body as a raw, uncontrollable fear overtook her. Mukesh's presence saturated the room with a palpable threat, his unblinking stare locked onto her with unsettling intensity.

"Riya," he said, his voice low and measured. "Are you alright?" The question seemed almost out of place, considering the situation. Riya gulped, her throat tight and parched. She paused, the silence stretching on for what seemed like forever, before answering, her voice trembling, "Y-yes... I'm fine. Mukesh?

Mukesh's expression shifted, confusion flickering across his face. "How do you know my name?"

Riya's hand moved to her face, her fingertips tracing the unfamiliar smoothness of her skin. A quiet gasp escaped her as she realized the scars had vanished. Her mind raced, struggling to comprehend the surreal situation. Was this just a dream, or had something far stranger unfolded?

Thinking quickly, she forced a nervous smile. "Oh! Ahh!... actually ... one of my friends mentioned you.", she stammered with confusion and concluded that's how I know your name.

Mukesh's confusion grew, his gaze sharpening as he studied her, his features betraying little. "I understand," he replied, his voice measured. "Then, could I get your number?"

The question hit her like a gut punch, and with it came a flood of painful memories. She remembered giving him her number, naively thinking it was nothing. But that moment had spiralled into a waking nightmare his numerous calls, the constant texts, his unsettling shadow following her everywhere. And ultimately, the assault that had left scars that went beyond the surface.

There she stood, facing an opportunity she hadn't dared to imagine. Her heart pounded fiercely, her mind spinning with a tangle of emotions revenge, justice, fear. But how could she possibly take that first step? Riya's lips parted, but the words refused to leave her mouth. Her mind raced a whirlwind of thoughts spiralling out of control. Then, as though something inside her snapped, she shot up from her seat, the chair scraping harshly against the floor.

"I... I have to go," she said, her voice a mix of panic and urgency. "I have an appointment with my professor. Excuse me." She didn't wait for his reply; she fled the room, her heart racing wildly. Mukesh's voice echoed behind her, confusion laced in every word, but she refused to look back. She sprinted, her legs carrying her faster with each passing second, though each step felt heavier than the last.

Riya quickly opened her eyes, her heart racing so fast. She sat up in bed, clutching the sheets tightly. The room was calm and still the shadows unchanged, and the air carried the faint scent of lavender from the candle she'd lit earlier. Riya realized it was just a dream.

The intensity of the moment was too lifelike the fear, the tension, the haunting sense of Mukesh's presence. Riya held her head in her hands fighting to bring her nerves under control. The clock beside her bed glowed 4:30 AM. Sleep was out of the question. With trembling fingers, she reached for her journal, opening it to pour out her thoughts:

"The dream was more than just a dream it was damn real. I'm certain of it. This is no coincidence; it's a message, a warning, or perhaps a challenge. Whatever it means, I must prepare. I must find strength. Justice is the only path ahead." Riya shut the journal with a decisive snap. The fight wasn't over. It was only just the beginning.

CHAPTER THIRTEEN

THE UNFINISHED BATTLE

Riya jolted awake, her mind flooded with vivid, broken fragments memories, emotions, and strange, unshakable images. Each one screamed for clarity, pulling at her from every direction. She didn't need reasons, these weren't just dreams. They were clues, tied to justice which she owed to herself and her late mother.

But where could she begin? Who would understand her? Clenching her fists, she resolved to act. The college library, her refuge of solace and answers would now become her battlefield. Pulling on her jacket, she stepped out into the unknown, a singular determination burning in her mind: I will uncover the truth.

The college library stood as a masterpiece of design, a serene haven with gleaming wooden floors, towering bookshelves stretching to meet vaulted ceilings, and stained-glass windows casting soft, colourful light across the room. As Riya entered, the comforting aroma of old books and ink welcomed her. Students sat absorbed in their studies, the gentle rustle of pages and hushed murmurs weaving a tranquil, scholarly atmosphere.

Riya approached the 'Psychology and Philosophy' section. Her fingers trailing over the spines of neatly lined-up books. Her eyes scanned titles like 'Dreams and Their Meanings', 'Fragments of the Subconscious, and The Secrets of the Sleeping Mind'. She picked out a few and carried them to a corner table by the window.

As Riya flipped through the books, she found theories about fragmented dreams how they might symbolize repressed memories or unresolved trauma. Some texts proposed that these pieces could be messages from the subconscious, guiding one to uncover hidden truths. A book named 'Dreams: A Gateway to the Truth' particularly stood out. It explored how recurring fragments could be tied to real-life events, encouraging the dreamer to face buried secrets.

Absorbing the information, her phone buzzed with a notification. It was a message from the college administration: "Reminder: Practical exams starting next week." A wave of anxiety swept over her. The realization hit hard time was running out, not just for exam preparation, but also for pursuing the justice her heart longed for. With resolve, she decided to divide her time, balancing both duties as best as possible.

Exhausted from hours of studying, Riya needed a break. The cafeteria, alive with voices, the clink of silverware, and the inviting fragrance of coffee, beckoned her for a short escape. She ordered a coffee and settled into a quiet corner, allowing her mind a brief rest.

Her moment of peace was fleeting. From across the room, she caught sight of Mukesh, effortlessly charming as he laughed with another girl. The sight sparked a storm of emotions sorrow, fury, and an intense urge to shield the girl from Mukesh's deceit. She knew the type of man he was, and the thought of someone else becoming a victim of his lies stung deeply.

As if on cue, Mukesh lifted his gaze, and their eyes locked. The air between them thickened with an unspoken tension, crackling like electricity. His face darkened into a frown, but Riya, burning with suppressed anger, stood her ground. With slow, deliberate movements, she pulled off her scarf, exposing the scar he had once given her. Her eyes, sharp and unyielding, bored into him with a silent accusation.

Mukesh hesitated, the weight of her gaze forcing him to falter. His once unshakable confidence crumbled, and within moments, he looked away, his expression unreadable. Without another word, he hurried out of the cafeteria, unable to bear the intensity of the moment.

For Riya, it was a small triumph, a chink in Mukesh's otherwise impenetrable armour. But she wasn't finished. Making sure he was out of sight she walked over to the girl. "Hey!" Riya began cautiously, her voice steady but urgent. "You don't know me, and I don't know you, but I know Mukesh all too well. Just... be careful around him. That's all I'm going to say."

The girl's eyes narrowed, a mix of confusion and defiance flashing across her face. "Why?" she snapped. "Are you jealous because Mukesh doesn't care about you anymore? He's already told me everything about you."

Riya's anger ignited. The audacity of Mukesh to manipulate and twist the truth yet again! She realized arguing would be pointless—Mukesh had already planted his lies. Without another word, she turned on her heel and walked away, her fists clenched, her resolve burning brighter than ever. Back in the library, Riya sank into her chair, her emotions still churning. She knew exposing

Mukesh's true nature would be anything but easy. Yet, the confrontation had only solidified her determination. Justice wasn't just an aspiration it had become her mission.

That moment marked the start of a new chapter in Riya's fight. Though minor, her first victory in shaking Mukesh's confidence fuelled her courage to press on—for herself, for her mother, and for the truth that demanded to be revealed.

CHAPTER FOURTEEN

Bites of the Past

Riya returned home after a gruelling day and sank into her favourite spot by the window. The her setting sun painted her room in shades of amber, while a soft breeze whispered through the leaves outside. With a steaming cup of chai in hand, its cardamom scent calming her weary mind, she let her gaze drift to the world beyond the glass. Her thoughts meandered peacefully until the buzz of phone broke the silence.

A message from her dad lit up the screen: "Riya, I'll be late tonight. Don't wait up. Have dinner, alright?" Riya smiled faintly at his care but felt a pang of loneliness. She decided she wouldn't settle for leftovers or takeout. Instead, she wanted to cook something comforting, something that would remind her of home. Heading to the kitchen, she recalled her mother's simple yet magical recipe 'Chitlam Podi'.

Chitlam Podi was a childhood favourite- a nutty, spicy powder made of roasted groundnuts, dried chilies, garlic, and cumin. Her mother had always said it was a "hug in food form," and tonight, Riya needed just that. She quickly gathered the ingredients, her hands moving almost instinctively as she roasted the groundnuts, their earthy aroma filling the kitchen.

As Riya ground the roasted ingredients in a mortar and pestle, the rhythmic sound transported her back to her childhood. She could almost see herself, a little girl sitting cross-legged on the kitchen floor, eyes wide with anticipation as she watched her mother work her magic.

"Ma, is it ready now?", young Riya would ask. Her stomach growling loudly enough to make them both laugh. "Patience, my little one!" her mother would say, her eyes sparkling with gentle mischief. "Good things take time, and the best flavours demand it." Then, with the kind of smile that felt like sunshine, she'd tear off a piece of warm chapatti, spread a dollop of butter that melted instantly, and dust it with freshly ground Chitlam Podi.

She'd hand it to little Riya, whose tiny hands could barely hold back their excitement. That first bite was always magical love made tangible in the simplest, most soulful way. Lost in the warmth of her memories, Riya began kneading the dough for the chapatti, her hands moving with practiced ease. She rolled it out into a perfect circle and laid it on the sizzling tawa. As the butter melted over the freshly cooked roti, its rich, inviting aroma filled the kitchen.

With care, she spread a generous layer of Chitlam Podi onto the roti, rolled it tightly into a cozy wrap, and set it neatly on a plate. Beside it, she placed a tall glass of chilled lassi, its frothy sweetness the perfect companion to the spicy, nutty wrap.

Sitting by the window once again, Riya took her first bite of the roll. The buttery softness of the chapatti paired with the nutty, tangy spice of the Podi sent waves of comfort through her. Each bite was a journey back in time. She sipped her lassi in between, the creamy sweetness perfectly balancing the flavours.

Sitting with her mom under the starry sky as her mother pointed out constellations and spun magical stories about them. 'That one!' her mom would say, pointing at Orion, "It's a brave warrior guarding the universe." Little Riya would listen, captivated, asking endless questions about the stars.

They would play endless games together, giving names to the stars, finding whimsical shapes in the clouds, and weaving imaginative stories for each one. Those moments were a treasure trove of laughter, pure, unfiltered joy and innocence that Riya now longed for with all her heart.

As she sipped her lassi, her gaze drifted outside. The patter of raindrops against the window caught her attention, and she realized it had started raining heavily. The sight of the rain awakened a flood of memories. Rainy days had always held a special charm in their home. At the first drops, her mom would dart into the kitchen to whip up 'Palam Puri', golden fritters made from ripe bananas. The tantalizing aroma of mashed bananas blended with cardamom, sizzling in hot oil, was a fragrance Riya had come to equate with unbridled joy and cozy contentment.

She could almost hear her mother's cheerful call, "Riya, hurry! The first batch is done!" Little Riya would perch by the counter, her eyes gleaming with anticipation, as the first warm, golden fritter was placed before her. Outside, the rain played its familiar melody, a rhythmic backdrop to their cozy ritual.

Now, though the kitchen was silent and her mother absent, the rain still felt like a gentle embrace. It carried her mother's love, woven into every cherished memory of those rainy-day traditions. Finishing her meal, Riya felt both comforted and nostalgic. She took her diary from the desk, the leather cover smooth under her fingers, and opened it to a fresh page.

Dear Ma,

Tonight, I made your 'Chitlam Podi'. Every bite reminded me of your laughter, your stories, and the love you put into every meal. As I sat by the window eating and sipping lassi, it started raining, and I couldn't help but think of you rushing to make 'Palam Puri'. I miss those moments, Ma. The way you made rainy days special with just a handful of bananas and your magic.

I miss the warmth of your voice and the sparkle in your eyes when you'd tell me stories about the stars. The house feels so quiet without you, but tonight, through the food and the rain, it felt like you were here with me. Thank you for leaving me these memories of your recipes, your stories, and your love.

I love you, Ma.

-Riya

As Riya closed her diary and set it on her nightstand, she looked out at the rain one last time. The rhythm of the droplets lulled her into a peaceful calm, and with her heart full of cherished memories, she slipped into bed, feeling closer to her mother than she had in long time.

CHAPTER FIFTEEN

THE TURNING POINT

Riya sat still in her room. Her eyes fixed on the blank, pale walls that seemed to echo her silence. The coldness in the air crept into her, making her shiver as she hugged herself for warmth. Slowly, she stood, reached for her favourite sweater a soft, worn piece that had once belonged to her mother and slipped it on.

As Riya slipped into bed, an unexpected warmth washed over her, soft and enveloping, as if an unseen hand had draped her in a tender embrace. It wasn't just a feeling it was a presence, vivid and reassuring, as though her mother was right there beside her. She could almost hear the familiar cadence of her mother's voice, spinning one of her magical bedtime stories. The comfort was so real, so vivid, it felt like love itself had taken shape to hold her through the quiet night.

For the first time in days, sleep claimed Riya with ease, wrapping her in a blanket of peace she hadn't felt in ages. But as her eyes blinked open, the room around her was unfamiliar, a world far removed from her own bedroom. Riya blinked, her vision sharpening as her surroundings began to take shape. She was in her college library, surrounded by the towering shelves of the Medical Sciences section. Rows upon rows of hefty textbooks on anatomy, pharmacology, and pathology loomed around her, their spines lined with years of knowledge. The air carried a distinct blend of aged paper and the crisp sterility of newly printed journals. A dim, diffused light filled the room, casting elongated shadows that gave the space an otherworldly feel. The chill in the air was eerily familiar, a reflection of the cold she'd felt before slipping into bed. Then she looked down at herself and froze.

She was still wearing the sweater she'd pulled on before bed, its familiar softness grounding her in the surreal moment. Her breath quickened as the truth began to sink in: this wasn't a simple dream. Somehow, through the veil of sleep, she had been carried back in time. The library, the sweater it all felt too vivid, too tangible to dismiss as mere fantasy. Her heart thundered in her chest as a single, electrifying thought took hold: This is it. My chance to rewrite everything.

Mukesh appeared before Riya could fully process her situation, she noticed movement at the edge of her vision. Mukesh was there, standing near a shelf filled with medical journals, watching her intently. His piercing gaze tried to lock onto hers, but this time, Riya wasn't the same naïve girl she had been before.

Determined not to let her emotions betray her, she quickly averted her eyes and picked up a heavy book on clinical diagnosis, flipping through its pages with purpose. Mukesh began to approach, his footsteps deliberate, his demeanour confident. But Riya wasn't about to let him get the upper hand.

She gathered her courage and walked briskly toward the digital library section, where rows of computers and e-books on advanced medical topics awaited. The hum of computers filled the air as she sat down and began searching for topics related to her coursework. Mukesh followed her, his presence like a shadow she couldn't shake. But she had made up her mind this time, she would not allow him to manipulate her or cloud her judgment.

As Riya browsed through research articles on cutting-edge surgical techniques and the latest medical advancements, Mukesh settled into the chair next to her. His presence was unmistakable, but she deliberately ignored him. Her eyes stayed fixed on the glowing screen, absorbing fragments of information about case studies and uncommon diseases, determined to keep her focus intact.

"Riya," Mukesh began, his voice low but insistent. She didn't respond. "Riya," he tried again, leaning closer. Still, she ignored him, her fingers continuing to navigate the medical e-library interface. Mukesh shifted in his seat, clearly unnerved by the cold shoulder. His impatience grew as he attempted to catch her gaze, but Riya, without hesitation, turned toward him. The expression on her face wasn't just a frown, it was a sharp, unwavering glare that spoke volumes, making her feelings unmistakably clear.

Her gaze locked onto his with unyielding intensity, never wavering. Mukesh's usual composure cracked under the weight of her stare. He fidgeted with his hands on the table, his eyes flitting nervously around the room, as though searching for a way out.

Unable to endure the silent standoff any longer, Mukesh finally stood and walked away. Riya's frown remained fixed until he was out of sight. Only then did she exhale a deep breath, her shoulders sagging in relief. She felt a glimmer of victory, a small but significant step toward regaining her strength and rewriting the course of her life.

Just as a sense of satisfaction began to settle over her, the shrill sound of her alarm sliced through the quiet of the library. Riya snapped awake, her heart racing, only to find herself back in her own bed. She sat up, disoriented, blinking as the soft morning light streamed through her window.

It took a moment for Riya to fully process what had just occurred. The library, Mukesh, the confrontation it all seemed so real, so detailed, as though she had truly lived it. She ran her fingers over the sweater still draped around her, and an unexpected warmth spread through her chest.

This dream wasn't just a random trick of the mind, she realized. It was something more. A sign, perhaps, that things were beginning to shift in her favour that the path ahead was no longer as uncertain as it once seemed. With a surge of determination, Riya leapt out of bed, dressed swiftly, and readied herself for the day. The feeling that something pivotal was about to unfold lingered in her mind. As she stepped outside into the cool morning air, a sense of purpose washed over her. She headed to college with newfound confidence, her resolve unshakable. This time, she was prepared to confront any obstacles that came her way, and she was certain she wouldn't falter.

CHAPTER SIXTEEN

IN EVERY STICH, IN EVERY BITE

The warm sunlight streamed through the window, casting a gentle glow on the calendar hanging on the wall. Riya's eyes slowly opened, and as they landed on today's date, it had hit her birthday. But instead of feeling excitement, a deep ache settled in her chest. It was her first birthday without her mother. She sat on the edge of the bed, fixated on the calendar, the vibrant morning light doing little to ease the heaviness that weighed on her heart.

"What's the point of celebrating without her?", She whispered, her voice barely audible in the stillness of the room. Determined not to let the sorrow overwhelm her, Riya rose from the bed and began to prepare for the day. After a quick shower, she stood before her wardrobe, her fingers gliding through the neatly arranged clothes. Her hand came to rest on a simple dress, one that her mother had lovingly stitched. In the past, she had often passed over these handmade garments in favour of store-bought ones. But today, the fabric felt different it seemed to hold a piece of her mother within it. She slipped it on, the gentle embrace of the material offering a quiet, comforting solace.

As Riya moved toward the kitchen, her phone buzzed. It was her father calling. "Good morning, Riya.", he said. His voice tender yet tinged with melancholy. "Come to the kitchen. I have prepared something for you."

She walked into the dining room and found him standing by the table, a plate of Kesari placed carefully at the centre. The rich golden hue of the dessert sparkled in the light, its sweet, inviting aroma sweeping her into a flood of memories. It was the same dish her mother had always made on her birthdays, each bite a reminder of the love that had gone into its preparation.

"I tried my best." her father said, his voice thick with emotion. "I wanted today to feel... special for you." Riya scooped up a spoonful of Kesari, the familiar taste hitting her instantly. The sweetness wrapped around her like a warm embrace, and for a moment, she let herself get lost in the memory. She remembered her mother in the kitchen, standing with a satisfied smile as she added the final touch to the dish, carefully tasting it to ensure it was just right. The image of her mother beaming when Riya savoured every bite was so vivid that it almost felt like she was there again.

Her eyes welled with tears, and before she could stop herself, they spilled down her cheeks. "It's perfect, Papa!" she whispered, her voice breaking as she threw her arms around him, holding onto the moment, to the love that still lingered in the air. Just as Riya wiped away the last of her tears, the doorbell chimed, pulling her from the moment. She opened the door to find Sandhya standing there, her hands full of a brightly wrapped gift, her smile as warm as ever.

"Happy birthday, Riya!" Sandhya beamed her energy almost tangible as she stepped inside.

Riya tried to force a smile, but the sadness that lingered in her eyes was impossible to mask. Sandhya noticed immediately and, with a soft, understanding look, handed her the gift. "Go on, open it," she coaxed gently, her voice full of care.

Riya hesitated, her heart heavy with the weight of the day, unsure if she was ready to embrace anything that felt too celebratory. But Sandhya's gentle persistence cut through the doubt. "Trust me, Riya. You're going to love this.", she urged softly.

Riya exhaled deeply her hands unsteady as she carefully removed the wrapping paper. As each layer fell away, her heart began to race, and when the gift was fully revealed, it took her breath away. There, before her, was a pencil sketch a strikingly intricate portrait of Riya and her mother, captured in a tender, peaceful moment. The strokes of the pencil seemed to breathe life into the memory, and for an instant, it felt as if her mother was right there beside her, smiling softly. The resemblance was so vivid, so real, that Riya could almost hear her mother's voice again.

The sketch captured one of Riya's most cherished memories: her mother enveloping her in a warm embrace after a school performance, her face glowing with pride. The level of detail was astonishing- the sparkle in her mother's eyes, the intricate draping of her saree, and the careful shading that breathed life into the moment.

Riya stood there, unable to tear her gaze away, her heart swelling with emotions that fluctuated between disbelief, wonder, and profound gratitude. Tears began to flow freely as she held the frame close to her chest, her voice breaking as she tried to speak. "Sandhya... I don't even have words.", she whispered, her emotions too powerful to be contained.

Sandhya smiled softly. "I knew how much you missed her. I just wanted to give you something to remind you that she's always with you." Without a word, Riya hugged Sandhya tightly, holding the portrait between them.

The rest of the day felt lighter. The Kesari, the dress, and the portrait each brought her mother's love back to her in unique ways. Later that evening, Riya sat by her window, the portrait propped up beside her. The sky was painted in shades of orange and purple as the sun dipped below the horizon.

She traced her fingers over the sketch, a bittersweet smile on her lips. For the first time in weeks, she felt not just the sting of loss but also the warmth of love. Her mother might not be there physically, but her presence lingered in the sweet taste of Kesari, in the stitches of her dress, and now in a portrait that Riya would treasure forever.

CHAPTER SEVENTEEN

A GIFT FROM THE PAST

The next morning, Riya woke up to an unexpected sense of calm. The sunlight poured into her room, its warm rays caressing the portrait of her mother, bringing the image to life once more. She sat up slowly, her gaze lingering on the portrait with a gentle smile. The events of her birthday had shifted something inside her, filling her with a renewed sense of purpose her mother's love, she realized, would always be her guiding light.

As she prepared for college, the dress her mother had so lovingly stitched felt like an embrace, wrapping her in the comfort of her mother's presence. She slipped it on, pairing it with a pendant her mother had gifted her years ago. When she looked in the mirror, she saw something different in her reflection—a quiet strength, an unspoken resolve in her eyes. The sparkle was back, brighter than before, as if she was ready to step into the world once again, carrying her mother's love with her every step of the way.

Riya was about to leave when the doorbell rang. It was the postman holding a small, weathered envelope. The handwriting on it made her heart skip a beat it was her mother's. "How is this possible?", she murmured, her fingers trembling as she accepted it. Riya shut the door behind her and sat down at the dining table, staring at the envelope. She hesitated, her heart racing with anticipation and fear. Finally, she opened it, revealing a neatly folded letter.

The words seemed to leap off the page:

"My Dearest Riya,

"If you're reading this, it means I am no longer with you. I wrote this letter for your 21st birthday, because I knew you might need my words now more than ever. Life has a way of overwhelming us, my love, but always remember that you carry my strength within you. I've left something for you—a piece of me that will always guide you. It's waiting for you inside the red trunk in the attic. With all my love, Ma."

Riya's hands trembled as she clutched the letter, her mother's familiar handwriting blurring through her tears. Her heart raced, a rush of emotions flooding her. The idea of her mother's words being there, waiting to offer some form of comfort, gave her a sense of urgency. She had never seen the red trunk before, but now, the need to find it felt like an undeniable pull. With every heartbeat, Riya knew she had to uncover whatever secret her mother had left for her, something that could change everything.

Riya rushed up to the attic, her breath quickening. The attic was dusty and filled with old memories-- stacks of books, photographs, and knick-knacks from her childhood. In the corner, tucked beneath a worn-out quilt, she spotted the red trunk. It was small but intricately designed, with a floral pattern etched into the wood. Her fingers brushed over it as she slowly opened the lid. Inside, she found a collection of handwritten journals, a small wooden box, and an old photograph of her mother holding a new born Riya. Riya picked up the wooden box first. Inside, she found a delicate silver bracelet with her mother's initials engraved on it. She slipped it onto her wrist, feeling a surge of emotion.

The journals, however, intrigued her the most. The first page Riya sat cross-legged on the attic floor and began to read. The journal was filled with her mother's thoughts, advice, and stories from her life. One entry caught her attention immediately:

"Riya, you've always been curious about the stars. Do you remember the nights we'd sit under the sky, and I'd tell you that the brightest stars are our ancestors watching over us? You, my little star, have the strength to shine even in the darkest nights."

Riya closed the journal for a moment, the memory flooding back to her. She remembered those nights vividly lying on the terrace with her mother, counting stars and dreaming of the future.

As Riya flipped through more pages, she realized that the journals were more than just her mother's memories they were a guide, a treasure trove of wisdom and love that her mother had left behind. Riya carefully tucked one of the journals into her bag, determined to hold onto the wisdom and love her mother had left behind. As she stepped out into the bright morning, the silver bracelet on her wrist caught the light, its subtle gleam grounding her in the quiet strength her mother had always instilled in her.

By the time she reached college, a sense of tranquillity had settled over her, something she hadn't felt in what seemed like forever. Her steps were lighter, her thoughts clearer. The weight of the past few months no longer pressed down on her as it had before.

As soon as she met Sandhya, her eyes flicked to the bracelet, a knowing smile spreading across her face. "New accessory?" Sandhya asked, a hint of playfulness in her voice as she gestured toward the bracelet. Riya smiled softly, touching the bracelet as though the simple action connected her to something much greater than herself. "It's not just an accessory," she said, her voice steady with a newfound resolve. "It's... a reminder." Sandhya raised an eyebrow, curiosity evident. "A reminder of what?"

Riya hesitated for a moment, then looked Sandhya in the eye. "A reminder of strength, of love, of everything that's helped me keep going." She paused, her heart was swelling with gratitude. "My mom gave it to me before... well, before she left."

Sandhya's expression softened, understanding passing between them. "It's beautiful," she said, her voice quiet, yet filled with respect. "And so are you, Riya. You're carrying her with you, in everything you do."

Riya smiled, the bond between them strengthening as she realized that even in her mother's absence, she was never truly alone. Riya nodded, her eyes shining. "It's my mom's. I found it this morning." Sandhya squeezed her hand. "You look different today, Riya. Happier." Riya smiled. "I think I finally understand that she's still with me, just in a different way."

That evening, Riya sat by her desk, her fingers turning the pages of the journals one after the other. Each entry, every word, felt like her mother was speaking directly to her, offering comfort and guidance. With each page, Riya could almost hear her mother's voice, soft yet filled with strength, filling the space around her. The more she read, the more she felt the weight in her heart lighten, replaced by a sense of warmth and determination.

By the time the evening faded into night, Riya felt connected to her mother in a way she hadn't experienced in months. The absence was still there, but now it wasn't a void it was a space filled with love and memories that could never be taken away.

As she lay in bed that night, the journal resting beside her, she realized something that shifted her perspective. Her mother's memory wasn't something she had to mourn, it was something she could celebrate. Her mother's wisdom was still with her, guiding her every step, and she would carry it forward with grace and strength.

Riya's eyes closed, a sense of peace settling over her. The following day, she promised herself, would be the beginning of a new chapter. Not a chapter defined by loss, but one shaped by resilience, love, and the timeless lessons her mother had passed down to her. She would honour her legacy, not by holding onto the pain of her absence, but by living a life that would make her proud. For the first time in months, Riya fell asleep with a smile, the bracelet on her wrist glowing softly in the moonlight.

CHAPTER EIGHTEEN

THE DREAM IN BROAD DAYLIGHT

Riya's eyelids felt heavy as the droning voice of her professor echoed through the lecture hall. It had been a long, exhausting day in the anatomy lab, and she couldn't fight the pull of sleep any longer. Resting her head on her folded arms, she drifted off, unaware that another strange journey awaited her.

Riya found herself in an oddly familiar setting, the college campus, but something felt different. The sky was bright, the sun casting long shadows across the courtyard. Students milled about, laughing and chatting, but their voices seemed distant, like whispers carried on the wind.

She looked down and noticed she was still wearing her mother's tailored dress and the silver bracelet from the red trunk. Her heart skipped a beat. Am I dreaming again? Before she could make sense of her surroundings, a voice called out from behind her.

"Riya!" She turned sharply, her stomach dropping as she saw Mukesh standing a few feet away. His face bore the same smug smirk that had haunted her memories. But this time, she felt a strange surge of courage, as though her mother's presence was wrapped around her like a shield. Mukesh approached her, his expression darkening when she didn't respond. "You've been avoiding me. We need to talk."

Riya clenched her fists, her mind racing. Not this time, she thought. Without a word, she turned and walked briskly toward the library, weaving through the crowd. "Riya, stop!" Mukesh's voice grew louder, but she didn't dare look back. Riya dashed up the library steps, her breath coming in quick, uneven gasps. The familiar scent of old books and the cool air washed over her, providing a brief sense of refuge. Her eyes flicked around the room, landing on a secluded alcove by the digital library section. She wasted no time, slipping into the nook and crouching low behind a shelf.

Moments later, the sound of Mukesh's footsteps echoed through the library, growing louder with each passing second. His presence was unmistakable as his figure moved past the rows of desks, his eyes scanning every corner for her. Riya held her breath, her heart hammering in her chest. She could almost feel his gaze, each step bringing him closer. The sharp, deliberate click of his shoes on the tiled floor was the only sound that filled the silence, amplifying her anxiety. Mukesh hesitated for a moment, his eyes scanning the shelves before his gaze landed on Riya. His expression shifted from smugness to surprise as she stepped out from her hiding spot, standing tall and unwavering. The silence stretched between them, thick with tension.

Riya squared her shoulders, her heart pounding but her voice steady. "What do you want, Mukesh?", she asked, her words cutting through the air like a challenge. The usual arrogance in his demeanour faltered as he took a step back, seemingly caught off guard by her newfound confidence. His smirk faltered. "I just want to talk."

"I have nothing to say to you," she replied, with her icy tone. "You've done enough damage." Mukesh's confidence wavered under her glare. For the first time, she saw a flicker of uncertainty in his eyes. He took a step back, muttering something under his breath before turning and walking away. As he disappeared from view, Riya exhaled shakily. She felt victorious, even if her legs were trembling.

Suddenly, a hand on her shoulder jolted her awake. "Riya!" She blinked, disoriented, as Sandhya's concerned face came into focus. "Are you okay? You were mumbling in your sleep." Riya glanced around the classroom, the dream fading but its intensity lingering. The professor was still lecturing, oblivious to her brief escape from reality.

"I'm fine," Riya whispered, though her heart was still racing. Sandhya raised an eyebrow but didn't press further. "Alright, just don't let him catch you sleeping in class. You don't want to end up in trouble." Riya sat up a little taller, her fingers tracing the silver bracelet as she thought. The dream lingered in her mind, vivid and powerful. It felt like more than just a figment of her imagination it was as if she had glimpsed a stronger, braver version of herself. The fear that had once held her back now seemed distant, she felt ready to face whatever came next.

Maybe, she thought, this is my chance to start anew. The rest of the lecture passed in a blur, but Riya's mind was sharper than ever, piecing together the meaning behind her dream. She didn't have all the answers yet, but one thing was clear, her journey was far from over.

CHAPTER NINETEEN

UNVEILING THE PAST

The beam of her desk lamp created a halo around the open pages of her notebook, where hastily scribbled notes sprawled across the lines. Riya's research on dreams and their connection to reality had drawn her into a labyrinth of theories. Her mind buzzed with thoughts. "Could dreams truly transport someone to the past? Could they serve as a gateway to rewrite fate?"

The words on the page swirled together as a sudden wave of fatigue washed over her. Riya blinked, trying to push through, but the soothing quiet of the night proved too powerful. Her eyelids grew heavier with each passing second, and before she could fight it any longer, her head dropped, surrendering to the pull of sleep. The familiar shift of her world began once more.

The dream pulled her back, and she found herself standing in her childhood home. The air felt heavy, as if thick with secrets and impending doom. Everything was eerily quiet. She moved through the familiar space, her heart pounding, her senses on high alert.

Her gaze fell on her mother's room, the door tightly shut. The faintest trace of something dark seeped out from beneath it a thin stream of red. Riya's breath hitched. 'Amma?' she called out, her voice trembling. She reached for the doorknob, her hands shaking. As she turned it, the door creaked open. The sight that greeted her was something out of a nightmare. Her mother lay on the floor, lifeless, blood pooling around her. Standing over her, clutching a cloth soaked in crimson, was Mukesh's father.

"No!" Riya screamed, but her voice was lost in the void of the dream. Her mother's face was frozen in a mixture of fear and defiance. It was clear she hadn't gone down without a fight. Her sari was torn, and fragments of a broken vase lay scattered around her. "Your silence was a problem," Mukesh's father said coldly, wiping his hands. "But now, there's no one left to speak."

Riya's heart raced. She wanted to intervene, to scream, to stop him but she was a mere observer in this haunting replay of the past. The scene shifted once more, revealing another piece of the puzzle. Riya's mother stood before the college Dean, her composure unwavering despite the looming danger. "This evidence is enough to expose him," her mother said, her voice steady, each word a quiet declaration of defiance. "It's not just about me; it's about protecting my daughter and countless others who've been silenced."

The dean's face was unreadable as he took the folder from her, his fingers brushing over the confidential documents. He nodded, a flicker of something unreadable crossing his features. But unbeknownst to both of them, there was a shadow lurking in the corner of the room. Mukesh's father watched from the darkness, his eyes blazing with fury, his clenched fists betraying the storm brewing within him. His expression was a twisted mix of rage and cold calculation, knowing that this moment, this betrayal, could never be allowed to stand. The air felt thick with the weight of impending violence, the danger far from over.

Later, Riya saw him in her home, confronting her mother. "You shouldn't have crossed me," he snarled, slamming his hand on the table. "I won't let you silence me," her mother retorted. "This ends here." What followed was chaos. Riya witnessed the struggle, the vase shattering, the moment her mother fell, her head striking the edge of the table.

Riya woke up with a start, her body drenched in sweat. Her chest heaved as she gasped for air, the images still vivid in her mind. Tears streamed down her face as the reality of what she had seen sank in. Her mother's death wasn't an accident. It was a calculated act, a murder orchestrated by Mukesh's father. She sat on the edge of her bed, trembling. The dream had shown her everything her mother's courage, the confrontation, and the betrayal.

Riya awoke with a start, her body drenched in sweat. Her chest heaved as she gasped for air, the images still vivid in her mind. Tears streamed down her face as the reality of what she had seen sank in. Her mother's death wasn't an accident. It was a calculated act, a murder orchestrated by Mukesh's father.

She sat on the edge of her bed, trembling. The dream had shown her everything—her mother's courage, the confrontation, and the betrayal. As the room around her came back into focus, Riya knew one thing: this wasn't just a revelation. It was a second chance. If her dreams could transport her to the past, they might also allow her to intervene, to change the course of events.

Wiping her tears, she whispered to herself, "I'll make it right, Amma. I promise." The night was far from over, but for Riya, it marked the beginning of a mission to uncover the truth and seek justice. Determined, she set out to gather evidence, confront Mukesh's father, and honour her mother's memory by ensuring that the truth would finally come to light. With each step, Riya felt her resolve strengthen, knowing that her mother's spirit was guiding her toward justice.

CHAPTER TWENTY

THE RESOLUTION BEGINS

The morning sun crept through Riya's curtains, painting her room in shades of gold. But the light brought no comfort. Her mind was a whirlwind of emotions anger, grief, and determination. The dream had been too vivid, too detailed to dismiss as just her imagination.

As she sat with her cup of chai, the events of the dream replayed in her head. Every detail was etched into her memory: her mother's defiance, Mukesh's father's cruelty, and the haunting scene in her childhood home. She clenched her fists. This wasn't just about her mother anymore it was about justice, about putting an end to the cycle of abuse and silence. Her phone buzzed, pulling her out of her thoughts. It was Sandhya.

"Riya, are you okay? You seemed off yesterday," Sandhya asked, concern evident in her voice. "I'm fine, Sandhya. Just a lot on my mind.", she replied. Riya spent the day pouring over her research, delving into the science and metaphysics of dreams. She read about lucid dreaming, the connection between the subconscious and reality, and the possibility of using dreams to alter the past. The pieces started falling into place. "This isn't just a coincidence.", she muttered to herself. "These dreams are trying to tell me something. They're giving me a chance."

The clock struck midnight when she decided to take a break. Exhausted, she leaned back in her chair, her mind still racing. The lamp cast long shadows across her room as she let her eyes close, the weight of the day pulling her into slumber. This time, the dream came almost instantly. Riya found herself back in her childhood home. The scene was eerily familiar, but this time she wasn't just an observer. She was there, fully aware, fully present.

She stood in the hallway, her heart pounding as she approached her mother's room. The door was ajar, and she could hear raised voices. "You think you can threaten me?" Mukesh's father snarled. "I'm not afraid of you," her mother shot back. Riya's hands trembled as she pushed the door open. She saw her mother standing tall, holding the evidence against Mukesh's father. Her courage was palpable, but so was the danger.

"Amma!" Riya shouted, stepping into the room. Both her mother and Mukesh's father turned to her, their faces a mixture of shock and confusion. "What are you doing here?" her mother asked, her voice trembling. Riya didn't have time to explain. She longed for the evidence, grabbing it from her mother's hands.

"You won't get away with this," Riya said, glaring at Mukesh's father. He smirked, taking a step toward her. "And what will you do? You're just a child."

But Riya wasn't a child anymore. She was armed with knowledge, with the clarity of her dreams. She darted out of the room, clutching the evidence, her heart pounding as she ran. She could hear Mukesh's father chasing her, his footsteps echoing in the hall. Desperation fuelled her as she made her way to the front door, throwing it open and running into the street.

Suddenly, Riya jolted awake, her chest heaving. She was back in her room, the dream fading like smoke, but its impact lingering. This time, it was different. She hadn't just watched the events unfold; she had been part of them. And though she hadn't been able to save her mother, she had taken the evidence.

Riya sat up, her mind racing. If she could dream again, if she could return to the past, she could do more. She could warn her mother, protect her, and change everything. She grabbed her notebook, scribbling down everything she remembered. The evidence, the confrontation, the chase it was all crucial. "This isn't over.", she whispered to herself. "I'm going back. And this time, I'll save you, Amma!" The resolve in her voice was unshakable. Riya felt a glimmer of hope. The past wasn't set in stone, and she had the power to rewrite it.

THE SCAR OF THE PAST

Chapter 21: The Scar of the Past

Riya ran her fingers over the faint scar on her cheek as she sat in the shadowy confines of her room, memories of her encounter with Mukesh surging unbidden to the forefront of her mind. The scar, no longer just a blemish on her skin, had morphed into a testament to her endurance a symbol of the battles she had endured and those she knew still awaited her.

Her gaze lingered on her reflection when her father stepped into the room silently, his concern plain in the lines of his face. "Riya," he began softly, "I'm worried about you. You've been retreating into yourself, immersing in… peculiar research."

Riya's eyes flicked toward her laptop, its screen glowing with search results for altering the past and parallel dimensions. Her father paused, uncertainty clouding his expression. "I've come across some of the things you've been exploring. I really think you should consider speaking with someone. A therapist, maybe."

She exhaled deeply, her fingers grazing the scar again. "Dad, you just don't get it. I'm okay." You're not," he said firmly, his tone more determined. "You're barely sleeping, you're not eating well, and you're fixating on things that are beyond your control. Please, just... consider speaking to someone." Riya finally gave a reluctant nod, though she doubted any therapist could truly comprehend the gravity of her situation.

The next day, Riya sat in Dr Anand's office, the scar on her face catching the harsh fluorescent light. She noticed how his eyes flickered to it briefly before he began. "Riya," he said, his tone professional, "Your father tells me you've been having unusual dreams and that you're... troubled by certain events in your past."

"It's more than what it seems," Riya said, her voice strained. "These dreams they aren't just figments of my imagination. They feel like doorways to the past. And I truly believe I can change what already occurred." Dr Anand leaned back slightly, raising a doubtful eyebrow. "Change the past? Can you explain what you mean by that?"

Riya took a deep breath. "I've seen what happened to my mother. I've seen what Mukesh did to me. Everything goes back to him. If I could just... not meet him, maybe my life would be different. Maybe my mom would still be alive."

Dr Anand's face turned grave at the mention of Mukesh. "Riya, are you suggesting Mukesh caused that scar?" Yes! she whispered, her voice unsteady. "And his father silenced everyone who tried to help me. He's powerful, above the law. But this isn't just about the scar it's everything he's destroyed in my life and my family's. I need to undo it all." Dr Anand tapped his pen against his notepad, clearly unsettled. "Riya, you've been through trauma. That much is clear. But trying to change the past... that's not possible.

You need to focus on healing, isn't?"

"I don't need healing.", she snapped. "I need justice. Do you know what it's like to feel powerless? To know that someone like Mukesh can destroy your life and walk away untouched?" The scar on her face burnt as if reminding her of its origin. She clenched her fists. "This scar... it's not just a mark. It's a reminder of the day, I lost everything. And it's all because of Mukesh and his father. If I can stop that, I can stop everything."

Back at home, Riya opened her notebook, jotting down every detail of her dreams and the events that had led to her mother's death. She drew connections, trying to pinpoint the exact moment everything began to unravel. It all led back to one day, the day she met Mukesh. If she hadn't crossed paths with him, she might never have been scarred physically or emotionally. Her mother might still be alive. Her life might still be intact.

She stared at her reflection in the mirror, her scar almost glowing in the dim light. It wasn't just a mark of pain. It was a challenge. A call to action. "I'll not meet him," she whispered to herself. "I'll rewrite everything." Exhausted from her research, Riya fell asleep at her desk, her mind racing with plans and possibilities.

In her dream, she was transported back to her college days. Mukesh was there, his predatory gaze locked onto her. But this time, she wasn't the same Riya. This time, she was ready. As he approached her, she turned sharply, avoiding him. The dream shifted, and she was at her house, standing in front of her mother's locked room. Blood seeped from underneath the door, the metallic scent filling her nostrils.

Riya's mother's voice lingered in her mind, a distant cry of desperation. "Don't let him triumph, Riya. Don't let him rob you of everything." Riya jerked awake, her skin slick with sweat. Her fingers instinctively brushed the scar on her body, her determination steeling. Mukesh and his father couldn't have the upper hand. She would find a way to rewrite history, whatever the cost.

CHAPTER TWENTY-TWO

RECLAIMING FOCUS

Riya sat on her bed, the laptop still displaying an article on quantum theories of time. Yet, her attention shifted to her phone, where a WhatsApp notification flashed repeatedly. She tapped it open and found a message from her class representative:

"Semester Exams start next week! Timetable is attached. Best of luck!"

A heavy weight settled in Riya's chest. Her obsession with seeking justice had left her academic life in ruins. The calendar on her wall seemed to mock her, filled with unchecked deadlines, while her desk was a chaotic mess of unopened textbooks and ignored notes. "I can't let this be another failure.", she whispered, a surge of resolve filling her heart.

The scar on her face caught her reflection in the mirror. For a moment, she touched it, the familiar pain of humiliation and regret threatening to creep in. But then she shook her head. "No more interruptions.", she murmured. "This is my moment to prove my worth not to Mukesh, not to anyone else, but to myself."

With that resolve, Riya picked up her bag and gathered her books. She needed a peaceful sanctuary to focus, far from the echoes of her insecurities. The college library was her ideal haven. The library was silent, except for the gentle shuffle of pages and the occasional tapping of keyboards. Riya spotted a secluded table bathed in warm sunlight and laid out her books and notes. She had just begun to dive into equations and diagrams when a recognizable laugh disrupted her focus.

"Well, look who's trying to play the studious one," teased Priya, one of her classmates, strolling past with a group of friends. Riya paid no attention, keeping her gaze firmly on the textbook before her. "Hey, Riya," someone else added with a smirk, "Aiming for the top now? Bit late for that, isn't it?" Their snickers were abruptly silenced by the stern tone of the librarian. "Keep it down! This is a library, not a hangout spot."

The group mumbled to themselves as they awkwardly moved on. Riya permitted herself a faint smile and returned her focus to her studies. Their jabs wouldn't shake her resolve. As the evening shadows lengthened, Riya packed up her books and stepped out of the library. To her surprise, her father was waiting by the college gate.

"Dad?" she said, startled. "What are you doing here?", "I thought I'd pick you up today," he said with a warm smile. "You've been working so hard. Let's get you home safely."

Riya felt a lump rise in her throat. Her father's presence reminded her of her mother the way she used to wait for her with snacks ready after school. The ride to home was quiet but comforting. When they arrived, her father handed her a plate of freshly cut fruits. "Eat these while you study," he said, "And let me know if you need anything else."

Riya nodded, her resolve strengthening. She wouldn't let him down. The days flew by as Riya buried herself in her studies. She spent hours pouring over her notes, revisiting lectures, and solving problems. Whenever fatigue threatened to overwhelm her, she thought of her scar, her mother, and her father's quiet support.

Her classmates' ridicule no longer mattered. The whispers and laughs faded into the background as she focused on what truly mattered: reclaiming control over her life. When the exam week arrived, Riya was ready. Each morning, her father wished her luck with a squeeze of her shoulder and a packed lunch. Sitting in the exam hall, Riya felt a surge of confidence. The questions seemed manageable, the answers flowing naturally. With each paper she submitted, she felt lighter, as if shedding the weight of her distractions and doubts.

As the final exam concluded, Riya walked out of the hall and inhaled deeply. She had given it her all, and for the first time in ages, a sense of pride swelled within her. Riya's eyes glistened, but she held her head high. She wasn't done fighting, but for now, she had won a battle that truly mattered.

CHAPTER TWENTY-THREE

A GLIMPSE OF PEACE

Riya had barely finished her final exams when her father announced a surprise plan. "Pack your bags.", he said with a grin. "We're heading to Matheran for a few days." Caught off guard, Riya stared at him. "A trip? Now?"

Her father nodded. "You've been under so much stress lately. It's time to unwind. Though hesitant at first, Riya agreed, and soon they were on their way to the tranquil hill station.

The journey to Matheran was both refreshing and tiring, but as they neared the hill station, Riya couldn't help but marvel at its charm. There were no cars, just winding paths, horse-drawn carriages, and the soothing rustle of leaves in the breeze. Their resort was perched on a hillside, offering a stunning view of the valley below. By the time they arrived, the sun was setting, painting the sky in brilliant hues of orange and purple. Riya felt a flicker of relief, a weight she hadn't realized she was carrying starting to lift. "We'll explore tomorrow.", her father said as they settled in for the evening. "For now, just rest."

The next morning, Riya woke to the golden sunlight streaming through the curtains and the soft chirping of birds outside. The rhythmic clopping of horses' hooves in the distance reminded her of the journey they had taken the day before. She stretched lazily, her injured hand bandaged from a minor mishap during her exams throbbing faintly. Turning toward the window, she saw her father seated with a cup of tea, gazing at the misty hills.

"Morning, Dad!", she greeted, her voice still heavy with sleep. "Good morning, Riya," he said, smiling warmly. "How's the hand?"

"It's better!", she replied, flexing her fingers gently. "Thanks for this trip. I think I needed it more than I realized." After breakfast, they set out to explore the serene beauty of Matheran. The fresh mountain air and the lush greenery worked their magic, easing Riya's lingering stress. They visited Charlotte Lake, its tranquil waters mirroring the vibrant blue sky.

Sitting on a bench by the lake, Riya let the calm seep into her. "This place is incredible!", she murmured, her eyes fixed on the gentle ripples. "It's what you needed.", her father replied, placing a comforting hand on her shoulder. Their exploration led them to a canopy walk, a bridge swaying gently over a dense forest. Riya hesitated, the height making her palms sweat.

"You don't have to do this if you're uncomfortable.", her father offered. But Riya shook her head. "No, I can do this." Step by cautious step, she crossed the bridge, her grip firm on the railing. Halfway across, she paused to take in the breath-taking view below a sea of green stretching endlessly.

When she reached the other side, she turned to her father with a triumphant grin. "I did it!" "I'm proud of you!", he said, beaming. "You've always been braver than you think." As the day wound down, they stopped at a viewpoint to watch the sunset. The sky was a masterpiece of fiery colours, casting a warm glow over the hills.

A little girl selling flowers approached them, and Riya bought a handful of vibrant marigolds. As the child scampered away with a grateful smile, Riya felt a strange sense of peace wash over her. "She reminded me of myself.", she said softly, twirling the flowers in her hand.

Her father glanced at her and smiled. "This trip was a good idea after all." Over dinner that evening, they laughed about the day's adventures, from the canopy walk to Riya's hesitation at riding a horse.

"Today I felt different," Riya admitted. "It's like I've finally let go of something that's been weighing me down." Her father reached for her hand and gave it a reassuring squeeze. "That's all! I wanted, to see you smile again." As Riya lay in bed that night, she reflected on the trip so far. It wasn't just a getaway; it was a reminder that she was capable of facing her fears, letting go, and embracing life again. After a long while, she felt truly free.

CHAPTER TWENTY-FOUR

REFLECTIONS AND REVELATIONS

"Morning, Dad!", she called out, her voice tinged with weariness. Her father turned, his face lighting up with a smile. "Good morning, Riya! How are you feeling today?" She replied flexing her fingers gently under the bandage, "It's better. The pain is manageable." Her father nodded. "That's good to hear. I thought we could spend the day exploring a bit, just some light walking and enjoying the sights."

Riya hesitated but then nodded. "Okay, let's do that. But no more horseback adventures." Her father chuckled. "Agreed." After a light breakfast of toast and scrambled eggs, the pair set out for a leisurely walk. The winding, cobblestone trails of Matheran unfurled before them, framed by tall, ancient trees whose leaves danced in the sunlight. The cool, fresh air was infused with the subtle fragrance of damp earth and blooming flowers.

As they walked, Riya felt an unexpected wave of tranquility washed over her. Her father paused now and then to draw her attention to the wonders around them a lively troupe of monkeys swinging from branches, a vibrant butterfly drifting elegantly, or the faint, soothing murmur of a distant waterfall. They arrived at a cozy café tucked away in the forest. Her father ordered tea and fritters while Riya marvelled at the charming decor- a blend of wooden furnishings, artistic hand-painted walls, and glowing lanterns.

"This place has such a unique vibe," Riya commented, savouring a sip of her tea. Her father smiled. "Sometimes, a new environment is all it takes to help us appreciate life's little pleasures. Their next stop was Charlotte Lake, one of Matheran's most serene attractions. The stillness of the water mirrored the lush greenery and the expansive sky above. Riya found herself drawn to the lake's edge, where she crouched to watch small ripples form and fade.

As she stared into the water, her reflection appeared fragmented in the ripples. She noticed the faint scar on her cheek, a fresh mark from the accident. Her fingers instinctively reached up to touch it, her chest tightening with a surge of emotion. The ripples began to settle, and Riya's reflection became clearer. Suddenly, another face emerged in the water's surface her mother's. It was fleeting, like a vision, but unmistakable. Her mother's gentle eyes and soft smile seemed to look back at her, as if offering reassurance.

Riya gasped, stumbling backward slightly. "Mom..." she whispered, her voice barely audible. Her father, who had been standing nearby, noticed her pale face. "Riya? Are you alright?"

She blinked, the reflection gone as quickly as it had appeared. "I think I just saw Mom's face in the water." Her father's expression shifted, a mixture of surprise and something deeper grief, perhaps, or understanding. He placed a hand on her shoulder. "The mind can play tricks on us sometimes, especially when we're overwhelmed."

Riya nodded numbly, but deep down, she felt it was more than just a trick of the mind. Later in the evening, they visited a viewpoint renowned for its sunsets. The sky was ablaze with hues of orange, pink, and gold, casting an ethereal glow over the hills.

Riya leaned against the railing, her injured hand resting gently by her side. The sunset seemed to mirror her emotions intense yet calming, vibrant yet fleeting. Her father stood beside her, his face serene as he took in the view. "Beautiful, isn't it?" Riya nodded, her voice soft. "It feels like the world is slowing down, just for a moment."

They watched in silence as the sun dipped below the horizon, leaving behind a canvas of fading colours. Just as they were about to leave the viewpoint, Riya's father suddenly became agitated, glancing nervously around. Riya, sensing a shift in his demeanour, asked, "Dad? What's wrong?"

He hesitated, his gaze darting toward a group of people gathered near a small shack. A man in a dark jacket stood out among them, his face partially obscured by a cap. Riya's father's voice dropped to a whisper. "I think I know him." Riya followed his gaze and frowned. "Who is he?" Her father didn't respond, his lips pressed into a thin line. "We need to leave, Riya."

Riya's heart pounded in her chest as she watched her father's face tense. Something was wrong he wasn't himself. That night, back at the resort, Riya found herself unable to sleep. Her mind raced with questions about the man her father seemed to recognize. The unease from earlier had not subsided.

Suddenly, she heard a soft knock at the door. Her father answered it, and Riya could hear muffled voices. Slipping quietly from her bed, she moved closer to listen. Through the crack, she saw her father speaking to the man from the viewpoint, the one with the dark jacket. Her heart thudded in her chest as she strained to hear. "I didn't expect her to be here," the man said in a low, firm voice. "But she's involved now. You need to tell her the truth."

Her father's voice was urgent, almost pleading. "Not yet. I can't. It's too dangerous." The door closed softly, leaving Riya frozen in place, her mind swirling with unanswered questions.

CHAPTER TWENTY-FIVE

WHISPERS IN THE CALM

"The morning arrived with an air of calm, as if the world had momentarily halted to reflect on the events of the night before. Riya awoke to the soft chirping of birds outside her window, their gentle tune barely concealing the lingering tension within her.

Her father was already up, sitting at the small table with a cup of tea in his hands. His eyes seemed softer, the tension from the night before replaced by a quiet resolve. "Good morning, Riya," he said, offering her a faint smile. "Morning, Dad." She paused, studying him closely. He seemed weary but calm, as if he had come to terms with whatever had happened.

After breakfast, her father proposed a brief walk around the resort. "A little fresh air might do us good," he said, his voice casual though his eyes remained attentive. The paths around the resort were quiet, lined with tall trees that swayed gently in the breeze. Riya found herself drawn to the serenity of the surroundings. It felt like the calm after a storm, and she let herself breathe a little easier. "Are you okay, Dad?" she asked after a while, her voice tentative.

Her father paused his gaze fixed on the horizon. "I am. And there's no need to worry, Riya. Life has its way of throwing challenges at us, but what truly counts is how we face them." His words were cryptic, but she nodded, deciding to let it rest for now. To shift her mood, her father suggested they explore the lively local bazaar. The air was thick with the scents of street food and the sounds of cheerful bargaining. Riya was immediately captivated by the vibrant stalls, each one bursting with dazzling jewellery, pretty dresses and beautifully carved wooden crafts, each piece seeming to have a story of its own.

She paused at a stall selling small trinkets and picked up a delicate bracelet adorned with tiny charms. It felt like a symbol of the simplicity she had been yearning for. "Do you like it?" her father asked, appearing beside her. Riya nodded, a small smile forming on her lips. "It's perfect." He bought it for her without hesitation, his own expression softening.

As the sun began to set, they returned to the resort and settled on the balcony of their room. The sky was painted in hues of orange and pink, and the air carried a soothing chill. Riya fiddled with the bracelet on her wrist, her thoughts drifting. "Dad," she began hesitantly, "I don't want to push, but... last night... Who was that man?" Her father exhaled deeply, settling into his chair. "He's an old acquaintance, someone I never thought I'd run into here". "Why was he here?" Riya asked softly.

Her father's gaze locked with hers, firm and composed. "He's here to stir up some things I thought I'd left in the past. But it's nothing you need to worry about. Riya wanted to press further but decided against it. For now, she was content with the honesty in his voice. That night, Riya stood at the edge of the resort's garden, her eyes lost in the vastness of the starry sky. The darkness no longer felt oppressive; instead, the twinkling lights above seemed to offer a quiet reassurance.

Her father joined her, his presence a steady anchor beside her. "You've grown so much, Riya," he said softly, his voice carrying an emotion she hadn't expected. "Stronger than you realize." She turned to him, taken aback by the tenderness in his words. "I've had a good teacher," she replied, her smile heartfelt and warm, the truth of it shining through. They stood in silence, the weight of unspoken words hanging between them. But the silence they shared was a comforting strength, a reminder that even in the face of uncertainty, there could be pockets of peace which could be small, fleeting, but enough to hold on to.

CHAPTER TWENTY-SIX

DOWN THE HILLS

The morning was filled with the soft hum of packing. Riya and her father moved through their room at the resort and they were folding clothes, collecting scattered items and methodically placing them into their suitcases. What had once been their temporary sanctuary now felt emptier, as if the memories they'd made had been folded neatly alongside their belongings. Riya zipped her suitcase shut and glanced out the window one last time. The view of the mist-covered hills filled her with a bittersweet feeling. This trip, despite its moments of chaos and uncertainty, had given her something intangible, a flicker of hope and a sense of clarity.

Her father stood at the door, suitcase in hand. "Ready, Riya?" he asked, his tone warm yet tinged with the same wistfulness she felt, "Yeah! I'm ready!" she replied, slinging her backpack over her shoulder. After days of uncertainty and reflection, their journey was drawing to a close. With their bags packed and their minds heavy with newfound thoughts, Riya and her father began the descent from the hill. The climb down the hill was slow and steady. The cobblestone paths, bordered by towering trees, seemed less daunting now. The cool morning air carried the scent of damp earth and wildflowers. Riya took a deep breath, savouring the freshness of it all. The path down was a quiet one, as if the land was offering them a gentle farewell.

As they travelled, her thoughts swirled. The events of the past few days - the accident, the moments of quiet reflection by Charlotte Lake, and the mysterious man her father had met had stirred something within her. She felt as though she were leaving Matheran with more than just memories. She carried with her a glimmer of hope, a belief that justice and change were within reach if she stayed true to her dreams.

"Dad," Riya said softly as they neared the base of the hill, her voice carrying the weight of new thoughts, "this trip... it made me realize a lot. I feel like I can actually make a difference. I want to try." Her father's gaze softened, a smile tugging at the corners of his mouth. "That spark has always been within you, Riya. I've always believed in you." Riya returned his smile, a sense of warmth settling in her chest, grounding her in that moment. The sense of possibility was real now.

The drive home unfolded quietly, the car navigating the winding roads before merging onto the highway. As the sun ascended, its golden rays stretched across the landscape, bathing everything in a golden light. Riya rested her head against the cool window, her mind tangled with the emotions of the trip the lessons, the challenges, and the unexpected moments of clarity. The steady hum of the engine, like a soft lullaby, began to settle her restless thoughts. Slowly, her eyelids grew heavy, and with a final, deep breath, she surrendered to sleep.

As sleep gently pulled her under, Riya once again found herself slipping into the dream world. She was back in the park the same one, yet different now. The vibrant colours that had once danced with life were now muted, shadowed by an eerie stillness that hung in the air like a thick fog. The familiar trees loomed ominously, their branches twisting like reaching fingers. Beneath the ancient banyan tree, Mukesh stood, his form partially hidden by the gnarled roots and thick foliage. His presence was as unnerving as ever, the air around him heavy with unspoken tension. His piercing gaze locked onto hers, cold and knowing, sending a chill racing down her spine.

'You can't run forever, Riya," Mukesh said, his voice low and menacing. Justice isn't always what it seems. Riya's heart raced as she clenched her fists. "I'm not afraid of you," she said, though her voice wavered. "I'll find the truth, and I'll fight for it". Mukesh chuckled, the sound cold and hollow. "We'll see about that," he said, stepping closer. The ground beneath her seemed to shift, the park dissolving into a swirl of shadows and light.

Suddenly, Riya's father's voice cut through the thick haze of her dream. "Riya! Wake up!" She jerked awake, her heart pounding in her chest, breath coming in erratic bursts. Her father's hand was on her shoulder, grounding her, his face etched with concern as he leaned closer. "You were shouting in your sleep," he said softly, his voice thick with worry. "Are you okay?"

Riya blinked, still disoriented, the horrors of the nightmare clinging to her like a shadow. She nodded quickly, though her heart thudded in her ears, a cold chill creeping up her spine. "It was just a dream.", she murmured, her voice barely a whisper, as if speaking louder would make the terror feel more real. She closed her eyes for a brief moment, trying to push the lingering fear away, but her mind remained tangled in the remnants of her nightmare.

Her father gave her a reassuring smile and handed her a bottle of water. "We're almost home. Try to rest a bit more if you can.'" Riya settled back into her seat her thoughts swirling. The dream lingered in her mind, its intensity still fresh. Mukesh's words echoed relentlessly, but instead of fear, they sparked a sense of resolve within her. She knew the road ahead wouldn't be easy, but she was ready. This journey had shifted something inside her, and she felt prepared for whatever challenges awaited.

As they finally arrived home, the sight of the house brought a wave of warmth and familiarity. Riya stepped out of the car, inhaling deeply as the sun sank beneath the horizon. She turned to her father and smiled softly. "It feels good to be home."

"It always is.", he replied, patting her shoulder. "But remember, home is also where your dreams take flight." "Riya nodded, her heart surged with determination.

CHAPTER TWENTY-SEVEN

REWRITING THE PAST

Riya felt as though she were imprisoned by the weight of her past, each memory a chain that bound her tighter with each passing day. The only refuge she had found was in her dreams. Every night, she slipped into a world where the past played out in vivid detail moments she longed to undo, instances when she had succumbed to the expectations of others, times when her silence had betrayed her true desires. Yet, now, as she revisited these haunting moments, the dreams had become her canvas, a chance to rewrite her story, to reclaim the parts of herself that had been lost in the shadows of regret.

That night, as Riya drifted into the dream world, she found herself standing once again in the heart of her college, surrounded by the familiar hum of classrooms, the laughter of students, and the soft rustling of pages being turned. It was a scene she knew well, a place she had visited countless times in her sleep. But this time, something was different. The air felt charged, as though the very walls of the campus recognized the shift within her. She was no longer the same Riya who had walked these halls before she had shed the skin of uncertainty, the girl weighed down by the expectations of others. Now, she was someone else. A version of herself forged by the lessons of her past, stronger, braver, and determined. This Riya had the courage to face the mistakes that had haunted her, the resilience to shape her future on her own terms.

In this very classroom, Riya saw Mukesh approaching her once again, just as he had in reality. His hands shook as he extended a bouquet of flowers, his eyes glimmering with anticipation. Riya had witnessed this moment unfold countless times before, and each time, she had responded the same way - reluctant, uncertain, hesitant to hurt him, yet too intimidated to confront her own feelings. In the past, she had accepted the flowers, forced a smile, and silently embraced his affection, despite her inner conflict. But that was then. Now, everything had changed.

In the dream, Riya made a different choice. She stared at the bouquet for a moment, then without a word, she turned her head away. The pain in her chest was sharp, but she felt a strange sense of liberation wash over her. For once, she wasn't bound by guilt or the fear of disappointing Mukesh. She was in control now. And in this world, where the past could be rewritten, she didn't have to fall into the same patterns.

Mukesh stood frozen for a moment, his face crestfallen, but he didn't speak. He simply lowered the flowers, his gaze drifting away. Riya watched as he turned and walked away, his shoulders slumped. The scene played out just as it had in real life, except now she felt a sense of power in her rejection, as though she had freed herself from the chains that had once kept her bound to Mukesh.

But the dream wasn't over. Later that same day, in the dream, Riya found herself alone in the cafeteria. Mukesh appeared once again, his face bright with hope, this time carrying a small box of chocolates. He stood in front of her, waiting for a response. The gesture was the same as it had been before, and Riya knew exactly how this would play out. In her past, she would have accepted the chocolates, unable to say no, even though she didn't want to. But not this time.

Riya stared at the chocolates on the table for a moment, then without a word, she stood up and left the room. She could hear Mukesh's voice calling after her, but she didn't stop. She didn't need to explain herself. She didn't need to make excuses. For the first time, she was choosing herself over his expectations, and it felt like a weight was lifting off her shoulders. When Mukesh entered the room a few moments later, he saw the chocolates on the table, untouched, and Riya was gone. He stared at them for a long moment, his confusion palpable. This was a version of Riya he didn't understand, a Riya, who was no longer bound by the old patterns, a Riya, who wasn't afraid to make the hard choices. In the real world, she had never been able to do this never been able to push him away when she needed to. But in the dream world, she was different.

Riya could feel the intensity of Mukesh's gaze, but she didn't let it affect her. She had come here to rewrite her past, and each time she rejected him, she felt more and more in control of her own narrative. This was the moment she had been waiting for. This was the chance to break free from the cycle of guilt, the cycle of pleasing others, the cycle of self-doubt.

But as the days in the dream went on, Mukesh's presence began to grow more oppressive. He would appear everywhere around corners, in classrooms, walking behind her on the paths of the campus. His obsession with her had never stopped, even after all the rejections. It was as though he couldn't understand that she had changed. That she was no longer the same person who had once quietly accepted his advances, too afraid to make him angry or upset. In her dreams, he was relentless, chasing her through the halls, calling out her name in desperation.

But Riya knew what she had to do. Each time he tried to approach, she would walk away, never looking back. She had been trapped in this cycle in her past, but now she was free. She didn't need to repeat the mistakes of the past, the mistakes of being passive, of allowing Mukesh's constant attention to make her feel trapped. This was her chance to change everything.

But as much as she tried to distance herself from him, the weight of the past still lingered. It wasn't just Mukesh's obsession with her that she had to escape it was the way she had allowed herself to be passive, to avoid confrontation, to accept the roles others had given her without question. The more she rejected him, the more she realized that this wasn't just about Mukesh; it was about her reclaiming control over her own life, her own choices.

In the real world, Riya had allowed herself to be shaped by the actions of others, but now, in the dream world, she was learning to rewrite her story. Every rejection, every choice to walk away, was a step toward freedom. She knew that in the waking world, she couldn't change the past, but in this dream world, she had the power to shape her future.

Riya wasn't merely escaping from Mukesh; she was fleeing from the person she had once been. With each step she took away from him, a deep sense of calm began to wash over her. This wasn't just a moment of rebellion it was her opportunity to reshape her entire existence. This time, she was determined that no one, least of all herself, would stand in the way of her transformation.

The dream world, with its surreal blend of familiarity and strangeness, became her sanctuary where the weight of the past no longer had any power over her. As she floated between sleep and wakefulness, she made a silent promise to herself. When she awoke, she would be someone entirely new. A Riya who had rewritten her own narrative, someone resilient enough to confront the future with confidence, leaving behind the mistakes that had once confined her.

A FEVERED AWAKENING

Chapter 28: A Fevered Awakening

Riya woke up the next morning with a dull ache in her body. It wasn't just the usual tiredness from a restless sleep, but something deeper, an exhaustion that seemed to seep into her bones. She groaned softly as she tried to stretch, but the pain only worsened. Her body felt heavier than usual, and a strange warmth radiated from her skin. With a sigh, she sat up, noticing that her head was spinning a little. Her breath came out in soft gasps, and the back of her throat felt dry. Something wasn't right. She touched her forehead, and the heat was unmistakable. A fever, she thought to herself, realizing it now. A wave of dizziness overtook her as she stood up, trying to steady herself. She stumbled slightly, leaning against the wall for support.

She shuffled toward the mirror, barely able to focus, but what she saw stopped her cold. The scarf she had worn for the past few days, the one her mother had given her was lying on the chair, no longer as vivid as it once was. It looked lighter, almost faded, as if time had worn it down. She blinked, rubbing her eyes, unsure if she was imagining things. Could it be? Was this another strange thing brought on by the fever? Or was it something more?

The feeling that her world was shifting, like the layers of her past and present were bleeding together, returned. Riya shook her head, trying to clear the confusion. But as she turned away from the mirror, she noticed something else, her room was much cleaner. The clutter that had once filled the space - books strewn about, clothes lying haphazardly was gone. The floor was swept, her desk organized. It was almost as if a new energy had entered the room overnight. The transformation left her speechless, too disoriented to grasp what was happening.

Riya took a few hesitant steps toward the door and made her way into the kitchen, still trying to shake off the disorienting feeling. As she walked in, the smell of something cooking caught her attention. Her father, usually not much of a cook, was standing by the stove, stirring something in a pan. The sight of him, hunched over with his sleeves rolled up, was strange yet oddly comforting. He looked at her, his face tense with concentration, and then noticed her standing there.

"Riya, you're awake?", he asked, his voice soft but full of concern. He seemed a little flustered, his eyes darting between her and the stove. "You're still feeling sick?", he asked. Riya nodded weakly. "I'm not feeling well, Dad. Just a bit of fever." Her father's face immediately softened, and he hurried over to her, his concern palpable. He gently placed a hand on her forehead, his brow furrowing as he felt the heat radiating from her skin. "You need rest, sweetheart!" he said, his voice gentle but firm. "I'll take care of you. You just sit down."

He gestured for her to sit at the kitchen table, and Riya, still dizzy, complied, sinking into the chair. Her father returned to his cooking, but this time his movements had an air of quiet purpose. She watched him, puzzled by how he had picked up the skill of cooking so effortlessly. Moments later, he placed a steaming plate of Poha in front of her. Her stomach growled at the familiar aroma, and a wave of nostalgia hit her. It was just like the Poha her mother used to make the same light, airy texture and perfect blend of spices. It had always been one of Riya' favourite dishes, and her mother's Poha had always wrapped her in a sense of warmth and security.

"Here you go!", her father said softly, sitting beside her. "I wasn't sure what you liked, but I remember your mom used to make this for you when you were younger." Riya blinked, feeling a lump form in her throat. She had never noticed before how much her father had tried to care for her in the little things, like cooking a meal she loved. As she took the first bite, the warm taste of Poha filled her mouth, and for a moment, she felt a sense of peace after a long time.

Her father watched her for a moment, then asked, "Why aren't you going to college today?" Riya paused, swallowing the food in her mouth before answering softly, "I'm feeling unwell, Dad. I think, I need to rest." He nodded without hesitation, his eyes clouded with concern. "Alright, no college today then. But you need to take care of yourself." He stood up and went over to the cupboard, retrieving some medicine and handing it to her along with a glass of water.

Riya swallowed the medicine with a soft sigh, appreciating her father's care. She took a slow, measured sip of water, then stood up, craving some fresh air to clear her mind. She walked to the balcony, stepping outside and leaning against the railing. Her eyes wandered to the bustling street below, but her mind felt distant, trapped in the fog of her fever. The sun hung high in the sky, bathing everything in its golden glow, but the weight of the heat was nothing compared to the heaviness pressing down on her body.

She watched as a group of kids walked to school, their little backpacks bouncing with each step. Some were crying, holding onto their mothers as they were scolded for being late. Riya couldn't help but think of her own childhood, of the mornings when her mother had been there to rush her out the door, her gentle voice calming her nerves. The sight of the children and their mothers made Riya realize just how much she missed her mother's presence, how she had always been there, taking care of every little detail, even when Riya had been too young to appreciate it.

Her thoughts drifted back to those days when her mother had stayed up late, tending to her when she was sick, gently pressing a cold cloth to her forehead and ensuring she had everything she needed. Riya could almost sense her mother's comforting presence now, even though she was no longer there. A wave of emotion surged within her, and Riya quickly blinked away the tears that threatened to fall. The ache in her chest felt unbearable. She longed for her mother's calming voice, for the solace only she could provide. But her mother was no longer around, and now Riya was left to navigate the challenges of life on her own.

After some time, her father came to the balcony, looking at her with a worried expression. "Riya!, he said gently, "You've been out here for a while. You should go rest." Riya nodded and reluctantly made her way back inside. She went to her room and sat down at her desk, the room still feeling strangely unfamiliar with its newfound cleanliness.

She picked up a book, but her mind was too clouded to concentrate. Her head felt heavier, and her body began to ache again.

As the day wore on, Riya's condition seemed to deteriorate. Her fever stubbornly clung to her, her body growing weaker with each passing hour. Her father, who had been trying to manage everything with a quiet resolve, finally decided to call the doctor. When the doctor arrived, his presence was steady and reassuring. He moved with purpose, his steps confident yet measured. After taking Riya's temperature, he frowned, his face betraying the concern he had tried to mask. "She's running a high fever," he said, his voice both gentle and firm. "She needs complete rest, and you must ensure she stays hydrated. I'll prescribe some medication to help, but we'll need to keep a cold compress on her forehead to help lower the temperature."

Her father acted swiftly, placing a cold cloth gently on her forehead. The coolness offered a fleeting sense of relief, soothing the fiery heat that had consumed her skin. He remained close, his presence a quiet reassurance. She could see the weariness etched on his face, the lines of concern deepening with each passing moment, yet he never left her side, as if he would do anything to ease her suffering. As the evening settled in, a soft glow from the setting sun casting shadows across the room, Riya's father prepared hot idlis' for her. The dish was simple, yet there was something deeply comforting about it, a gesture of care that spoke louder than any words. Riya ate slowly, each bite a reminder of her need for nourishment, not just for her body but for her spirit. The warmth of the food settled in her stomach, soothing her in ways she hadn't anticipated. When she finished, her body ached for rest, and she slowly made her way back to bed, her limbs heavy with exhaustion but wrapped in a sense of quiet gratitude. The unfamiliar weight of relying on her father stirred something within her, a mix of vulnerability and warmth that she hadn't felt in years. She had always been the one to take care of others, the one who had to be strong, but tonight, for the first time, she allowed herself to be taken care of. In that surrender, a softness bloomed inside her, something gentle and tender, a part of herself she'd long neglected.

She closed her eyes, the fever still clinging to her like an unwelcomed shadow, but for once, she didn't fight it. She let the weariness pull her under, drifting into sleep. Her dreams were distant, blurred fragments of her past and whispers of the future, but one thing stood out with a clarity that touched her heart she was no longer alone. There, in the haze of her slumber, she felt the presence of something more a quiet support, a reassurance that she could lean on, a reminder that she didn't have to face the world by herself anymore.

CHAPTER TWENTY-NINE

THE DREAM GAME

Riya's feverish body finally gave into exhaustion, and as sleep overcame her once again, she found herself transported back into the strange, shifting world of her dreams. She had become familiar with this world, where everything seemed both distant and vivid, where past and present collided in unpredictable ways. This time, she found herself standing in the college lab, surrounded by the sterile scent of chemicals and the quiet hum of activity. The setting was eerily familiar, a moment she had experienced before in her past, yet here, in this dream world, it felt as though she had the power to alter it.

Riya's gaze swept across the room, landing on the familiar figure of Mukesh. He stood at a distance, his eyes fixed on her, studying her every move. In reality, their interactions had always been filled with tension, with Mukesh persistently seeking her attention, crossing lines she never asked him to. But here, in the dream world, Riya was resolute not to slip back into the old patterns. She had grown from her past experiences, and now, this was her moment to redefine her story, to seize control of the narrative.

Mukesh, sensing an opportunity, took a few steps closer and flashed a smile, attempting to capture her attention. In reality, Riya had always struggled with his relentless persistence, but in this dream, she remained unshaken. She purposely turned her gaze away from him, her concentration solely on the task before her. She could feel the weight of his stare, but she refused to acknowledge it.

Noticing Riya's indifference, Mukesh's frustration grew. He fidgeted with his phone, dialled a number, and whispered into it, his voice laced with impatience. Riya could catch snippets of the conversation, though she paid it no mind. A moment later, his friend, seemingly aware of Mukesh's growing irritation, called out to her in a light, teasing voice, "Hey, Riya! Mukesh wants to talk to you!" The words hung in the air, but Riya remained unmoved, her focus unbroken, and her ignorance deeper than ever.

Riya didn't flinch, her gaze never wavering from her work. She had mastered this silent game, knowing precisely how to control the dynamics. Mukesh's friend, sensing her indifference, let out a laugh, her tone laced with mockery. "Guess she's not interested," she remarked, her voice heavy with sarcasm, a smirk playing at the corners of her lips.

Mukesh's face flushed a deep red with frustration, his jaw tightening in a mix of irritation and disbelief. He had always been the one to get what he wanted, his determination and single-minded focus unwavering. When he pursued something, he did so with an intensity that bulldozed everything in its path, undeterred by obstacles. His stubbornness and relentless were what defined him. Yet, in this moment, Riya was a force he couldn't bend to his will. She refused to give him the attention he craved, and the lack of control left him visibly rattled. This was the chink in Mukesh's armour: his belief that anything or anyone could be his, a belief that, when challenged, shattered the illusion of power he clung to. The loss of that control left him vulnerable, and for the first time, he didn't know how to regain it.

Mukesh's frustration reached its peak as his desire to break Riya's silence grew more intense. Without warning, he snatched a piece of paper from his desk, crumpled it into a ball, and with a sharp movement, hurled it in her direction. The paper landed softly in front of her, the message within unmistakably clear, "Meet me in the park at 4:30 PM, near the college."

Riya didn't even flinch. She didn't spare a glance at the paper, her gaze steady and unwavering. She wiped the sweat from her forehead with the back of her hand, as though Mukesh's antics were no more than an irrelevant noise in the background of her thoughts. She reached down and picked up the crumpled ball, not with curiosity, but with an air of indifference. She didn't need to read it to know it was an attempt at regaining control over her. Instead of acknowledging it, she walked over to the trash can, her movements calm and deliberate, and tossed it in without a second thought. There was no reaction, no tension just the quiet certainty of someone who had long since stopped playing his game.

The action was deliberate, an unspoken declaration of Riya's resolve. With that single motion, she communicated more clearly than words ever could. It was her quiet rejection, a firm statement that Mukesh's persistence held no sway in this space. His attempts, his demands, they meant nothing here. She had long since mastered the art of silence, wielding it now like a weapon, each moment of stillness more powerful than the last.

Mukesh's fury erupted. His face contorted with frustration, his jaw clenched, and his hands balled into fists, shaking with the strain of his rage. He stalked around the lab, his movements harsh and erratic, the sound of his footfalls pounding like a drumbeat in the silence. The air seemed to grow thick with his anger, the tension so palpable that even the walls of the lab seemed to shudder under its weight. For a fleeting moment, Riya felt a flicker of discomfort, the familiar unease creeping in as she recognized the storm building inside him. She knew him too well. He was losing his grip, unravelling, and it was only a matter of time before the eruption would come.

In his blind rage, Mukesh stormed past his friend, whose eyes were still gleaming with a mix of amusement and curiosity, watching the entire scene unfold like a spectator. But Mukesh's fury was uncontainable, his steps quick and aggressive, turning on a dime as he shot past the other. His sudden movement caught his friend off guard, and before he could react, the beaker filled with caustic chemical acid slipped from his grasp. Time seemed to slow as the beaker tumbled through the air, and the acid splashed outward in a cruel arc, landing directly on Mukesh's face with a sickening hiss.

A piercing scream escaped his lips as the acid seared his skin. He stumbled backward, his hands instinctively reaching up to his face, trying to wipe away the burning liquid. But it was too late the acid had already done its damage. The pain was excruciating. Mukesh's face contorted in agony, his eyes wide with shock and horror. The acid had splashed across one side of his face, leaving behind angry red burns that would surely scar. His cries of pain echoed throughout the room, the sound a stark contrast to the quiet tension that had preceded it.

Riya stood frozen, her heart pounding in her chest. The sight of Mukesh writhing in pain was unsettling, but she also recognized the consequences of his actions. He had pushed too far. His desire to control, to manipulate, had led him to this moment. The dream had allowed her to change the course of events, to alter her own reaction. But now, she had witnessed the outcome of his unchecked anger.

Mukesh fell to the ground, his body trembling as he wept uncontrollably, the tears streaking down his face, mingling with the remnants of the acid's burn. His sobs were no longer laced with rage, but raw, guttural cries of anguish and remorse. He had fallen from the pedestal he had once placed himself on, broken and exposed.

Riya remained still, her emotions a storm within her-sympathy for his pain, disgust for his past behaviour, and an almost bittersweet sorrow for the person he once was. But she didn't waver. This was her domain now, a world she held in her hands. She had long cast off the shackles of fear, and she wasn't going to let him regain control over her. She had chosen her path, and in her silence lay her power something Mukesh could no longer manipulate. As Mukesh's cries echoed behind her, Riya turned away, her resolve unwavering. She didn't know how much longer she could remain in this dream, but one truth stood clear: she had rewritten her past. In this fleeting moment, she had freed herself from the chains of old wounds and patterns that had once defined her.

The sobs that once pierced her with unease slowly faded into the distance, and the dream world began to dissolve around her like mist evaporating in the morning sun. But as her eyelids fluttered open, a deep sense of clarity washed over her. In this dream, she had taken a decisive step toward liberation. Though it was only a dream, the empowerment she felt lingered, a quiet promise that she was ready to move forward, unburdened, unafraid.

CHAPTER THIRTY

Stronger Than Before

Riya slowly began to rouse from her slumber, the remnants of sleep lingering in her bones, yet a strange stillness hung in the air. A cool sensation brushed against her cheek, drawing her attention. She blinked her eyes open, her surroundings slowly coming into focus. The ice pack, once firmly placed on her forehead, had slipped to the side. As her hand reached out to adjust it, her fingers grazed her skin. It felt different unlike the fevered warmth of before. Her skin was smooth, almost unnaturally so, as if it had been tenderly cared for in a way she hadn't noticed before. There was a softness to it, a subtle lightness that made her pause. The sensation felt like a quiet promise, a subtle reminder of the healing she had not only experienced in her body but in her spirit as well.

Her heart skipped a beat, a sense of wonder washing over her. Confused, she stood up quickly, her legs shaky, and stumbled towards the nearest mirror. She gazed at her reflection in disbelief, her fingers gently tracing her now flawless skin. There was no sign of the scar that had been there for as long as she could remember. The mark that had once defined her face, that had always been a reminder of her past, was gone.

A sudden wave of disbelief crashed over her, leaving her breathless. Riya spun around, desperately searching for someone, anyone, who could offer an explanation for the miracle she had just experienced. Her heart pounded in her chest as she bolted toward her mother's bedroom, but the room was eerily empty. She called out her mother her voice tinged with growing anxiety, but the silence that followed sent a chill down her spine. Panic crept up her throat, constricting her breath as her mind raced in frantic circles. Where could she be? What was happening? The absence of her mother felt like an unanswered question, leaving Riya feeling more alone than she ever had before.

Her mind was clouded with confusion, the uncertainty growing with every passing moment. Heart racing, she rushed downstairs, her eyes desperately searching for something anything that could explain the strange events unfolding around her. She found her father in the living room, absorbed in the morning newspaper, a quiet stillness surrounding him. His presence should have offered comfort, but instead, it heightened her anxiety. Her pulse quickened as she moved toward him, urgency in every step. She needed to share what she had discovered, to see if he could provide any explanation. The weight of the unknown pressed heavily on her, and she hoped he could offer the clarity she so desperately sought.

"Dad! Look at my skin! It's completely clear now! There's no scar!", Riya shouted, her voice trembling with a mix of disbelief and exhilaration. She stood there, her heart racing, her eyes wide with a desperate need for her father to recognize the miracle she had just experienced. Her words hung in the air, but her father's reaction was nothing like what she had imagined. He slowly lifted his gaze from the newspaper, his brow furrowing in mild confusion. "Did you do a facial or something?" he asked, his voice casual, almost dismissive. His tone lacked the astonishment she expected, the shock she felt deep in her bones.

Riya's heart dropped. She blinked, her pulse pounding in her ears. Did he not understand? She glanced at her reflection in the nearby mirror, her fingers almost trembling as they traced the smooth, unblemished skin. Was he not seeing what I was seeing? A cold shiver of doubt crept over her, the weight of the moment settling heavily on her chest. She had expected a response filled with awe, or at least some form of recognition. But instead, there was only indifference, a quiet distance between her and the man she had turned to for answers.

Confusion swirled in her mind, replacing the excitement with a creeping unease. Was this real? Had it all been a dream? Riya's mind spun, her thoughts in a whirlpool of confusion and disbelief. She couldn't fathom his lack of reaction couldn't understand how he could be so detached from the miracle unfolding in front of them. Her eyes locked onto his, searching for some trace of recognition, but all she found was an unsettling calm. It was as if he wasn't even seeing her, not truly.

Her breath caught in her throat as the weight of the moment pressed down on her. The room felt like it was closing in around her, the walls seemingly shifting as her heart raced. Her pulse quickened with a sudden, sharp fear. She could barely process the casualness of his words, her mind only able to grasp one thing now, the question that had been growing at the back of her thoughts, gnawing at her relentlessly. "Dad... where's Mom?" Her voice cracked, barely a whisper, filled with a tremor of panic she couldn't hide. "What happened to her?"

The words left her mouth before she could even fully understand them. The fear that gripped her chest felt cold, paralyzing. As if something was wrong, terribly wrong, and she needed answers for that, for reasons she couldn't yet comprehend, seemed to elude her. She searched his face, desperate for a hint, a spark of recognition, but there was nothing. Only silence hung in the air between them, thick with a sense of foreboding she couldn't escape.

Her father's face hardened, his eyes narrowing. He put the paper down slowly, looking at her as though she had asked an absurd question. "Why are you asking? You know already, don't you? Your mother passed away in that accident," he said flatly.

Riya felt her legs weaken beneath her. "No... What? No!" Her voice rose in panic. She could feel her mind spiralling, the ground beneath her feet giving way. How was this possible? Her mother couldn't be gone. It didn't make sense. None of it did. Her mind was a storm of confusion, each thought swirling chaotically, refusing to settle. She couldn't make sense of what was happening, her reality shifting in ways she couldn't grasp. Her heart raced as she scrambled for something, anything that could anchor her, something familiar. In a panic, she snatched her diary from the table, her hands trembling as she flipped through the pages with a sense of desperation. Each page was filled with her scribbles, her random musings, the fragments of her daily life. Nothing was different nothing except for her face. The scar, the mark that had been a part of her for as long as she could remember, was gone, erased as if it had never existed.

Her breath came in short, shallow gasps as the question reverberated in her mind: How? What happened? She pressed her hands to her face, her fingers trembling, as if touching it would offer some explanation. But nothing made sense. The reflection in the mirror, her father's indifferent response, the emptiness where her mother should have been it was all spinning out of control.

Her eyes closed tightly, and she willed herself to concentrate, to make sense of the madness consuming her. She tried to focus on her breath, steadying herself, but it felt like trying to catch smoke with bare hands. The world seemed to blur around her, slipping away, and yet she was stuck in this moment, unable to break free from the overwhelming uncertainty that had taken hold of her.

In a panic, Riya grabbed her phone, her hands shaking uncontrollably. She snapped a photo of her reflection, her flawless skin staring back at her, more perfect than it had ever been. Her heart pounded in her chest as she quickly sent the image to Sandhya, her closest confidante, praying for an answer, for some kind of clarity amidst the overwhelming confusion.

"See? I got my old skin back! There's no scar anymore!" she typed, waiting anxiously for a reply. Sandhya's response was quick, almost too casual. "Oh, come on, Riya. You had the same face before. When did you have a scar on it? It's Mukesh who has the scar on his face." Riya's breath caught in her throat. "What?" she whispered, her mind reeling with disbelief. She had always believed the scar was a part of her, her flaw to bear. But now... was it actually Mukesh's? Fragments of the past began to surface, but they felt jumbled, disconnected. "How... how could this be?" she typed back quickly, her thoughts spinning.

Within moments, Sandhya's response appeared, clear and direct. Wait "Did you forget what happened in the lab?" Riya froze, her breath catching in her throat as the weight of the realization hit her. Her stomach churned with a mix of disbelief and dread. The dream the strange, vivid sensation of change it was all coming back to her now. The accident. The lab. The moment her body had shifted, as though something deep inside her had rewritten itself. It wasn't just a dream. It had all been real.

Her hands shook as she stood up, a rush of urgency flooding through her. She couldn't waste another second. The truth was out there, and she had to find it. She had to go to college, now. She didn't know what she would uncover, but she was certain of one thing: whatever had happened, it had begun there, in that very lab. Riya quickly changed into her usual outfit, her fingers moving with a sense of urgency as if each moment held more weight than the last. When she stepped outside, the air felt strangely calm, almost surreal like the world was holding its breath. The quiet stillness pressed against her, amplifying the whirlwind of thoughts in her mind. Everything felt so disjointed, too much to process in one go, yet she couldn't stop herself from moving forward.

As she reached the college campus, her gaze immediately fell on Mukesh. He stood near the entrance, his posture stiff, and his face concealed behind a mask. The sight struck her like a bolt of electricity, sending an involuntary shiver down her spine. There was something about the mask that unnerved her, an eerie sense of distance and separation between them. As she walked closer, she could feel the weight of his discomfort, his eyes darting away whenever they neared hers. He couldn't meet her gaze, and that nervous tension was palpable in the air around him.

Riya felt an unexpected sense of calm sweep over her, as though the world had shifted into focus. Mukesh, once the symbol of her own insecurities, now stood before her with a mask hiding the very scar that had haunted him. It was an irony that struck deep within her she had carried the weight of imperfection for so long, only to realize it had never truly been hers to carry.

In that quiet moment, something inside her released. The invisible burden she had shouldered for years seemed to lift as she watched Mukesh, hiding behind his own mask, unable to escape the truth that had always been with him. The scar he once shared with her, and the insecurities it carried, now belonged to him alone.

A wave of clarity washed over her, sweeping away the confusion and turmoil that had once clouded her thoughts. The past, with all its shadows and echoes, no longer held her captive. For the first time in what felt like an eternity, Riya felt a newfound freedom free from the weight of old memories, self-doubt, and the insecurities that had long confined her. The burden that had once pressed down on her chest evaporated, leaving behind a sense of lightness that she hadn't known in years. Her heart beat with ease, her mind was unburdened, and for the first time, she allowed herself to fully embrace the peace that blossomed quietly within her.

The rain began softly at first, a gentle tap on the earth, but soon it grew heavier, its rhythm intensifying as it danced upon the ground. Riya sat on the park bench, her mind caught between the joy of silent triumph and the ache of missing her mother. And it hit her that there was no way to bring back the ones who had left. The weight of the past of things lost hung in the air, but she was learning to accept the reality. The droplets, cool and soothing, draped over her skin like a soft embrace.

Her heart, usually so burdened with unspoken pain, seemed to smile in the midst of the storm. She closed her eyes, letting the rain wash over her, as if it was cleansing not just her body, but her soul. A quiet, contented smile tugged at her lips. The world around her blurred in the peaceful rhythm of the rain, and for the first time, she felt a true sense of peace one that wasn't dependent on what had been lost or what could never return. This was the moment of release, the surrender to what was, and in it, she found the freedom she had long been searching for.